ROSE CONCANNON

Carolyn Rose Hall

ISBN: 1511719109
ISBN 13: 9781511719100

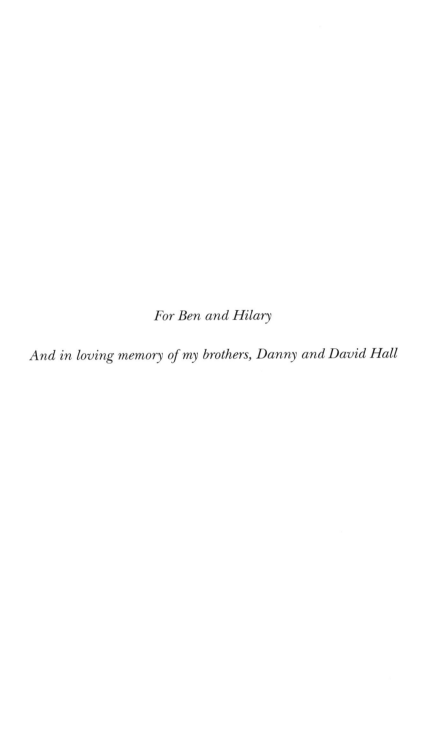

For Ben and Hilary

And in loving memory of my brothers, Danny and David Hall

I

The Things God Wants

1

LUCKY BABY

If we accept the things God wants of us, even when they are hard, the Holy Spirit will come to make them easy.

Baltimore Catechism: The Truths of Our Catholic Faith

The kitchen door opened and my mother appeared, wrapped in a long, brown plaid coat I hadn't seen before, with a green silk scarf knotted at her throat, smelling of the rainy morning and carrying a bundle of blankets in her arms.

I was making peanut butter and jam sandwiches for my brothers, my sister, Margaret, and me. I had to dig down to the bottom of the jar, where the peanut butter was hard and dry, and when I tried to spread it, the bread kept ripping.

Mother! I dropped my knife on the floor. *Mother!* I ran to her, afraid she might disappear if I looked away for even one second. She smiled, but before I could reach her and wrap my arms around her, my father hurried in, too, shaking the weather from his head like a wet puppy.

He carried a duffel bag on one arm and a soggy, brown-paper grocery bag in the other. The bag split when he set it on the kitchen table and the groceries spilled out. I wanted to check if there was peanut butter, but he stopped me. "Put the groceries away later, Rose. Come help your mother with the baby."

He was wearing a new leather coat, and I wondered where all the new clothes and groceries were coming from and I wondered if there was something for me. I started to follow him and Mother, but he stopped me again and pointed at the knife. "Rose," he said.

I snatched it off the floor, threw it into the sink with the other dirty dishes, and hurried to catch up with my parents. "Did you get me a new coat, too? Can I see the new baby? Mother, is it a boy or a girl?"

I hadn't known about the baby. Mother went to the hospital often for a rest, and I never knew when she would return. Usually she was gone for a few weeks, sometimes longer, and then suddenly she would appear at home again, busy and silent, like a moth at a lamp. How did it get in?

In the bedroom doorway we all stopped and stared at Mother's room—the unmade bed buried in clothes and towels, the empty cracker boxes and dirty dishes on the floor. "Me'n Margaret were sleeping here," I said.

Every time my mother was away, Margaret wet her bed. There weren't any clean sheets and my bed was too small for both of us, so I told her to sleep in here, but she was afraid to be alone, she has nightmares, so we had slept together in Mother's room for the last week. "Mother, I'll make the bed for you and the baby."

Dad dropped the duffel bag in the closet and said he had to take a nap before he went to work; he had a new job working the graveyard shift, so he slept in the basement now where no one could disturb him, not even Mother. "Try to be useful," he said.

"Mother," I said again as soon as he left the room, "is that a boy or a girl?" I started making the bed, hoping that if I took good enough care of Mother, she would stay home for good.

I turned the pillowcases inside out so they looked clean and white, and as I pulled them over the pillows I prayed to the Virgin that this was a boy so maybe the Catholic Aid Society ladies wouldn't take him away from us like they did my little sister Lucille. After Lucille left, Mother had sat in her rocking chair for a whole week, not eating, not sleeping, hardly even going to the bathroom, until Father and Aunt Mollie took her to the hospital.

"There." I plumped and patted the pillows and smiled at Mother, sitting in her rocking chair, feeding the baby from her breast and softly singing some song I knew I had heard before, but the song was not for me. That lucky little baby was breathing in her sweet mother smell. I tiptoed back to the kitchen.

Tommy was sitting on the floor with a new jar of peanut butter in his lap, scooping it into his mouth and smearing it all over his face with his filthy fingers. All he was wearing was a damp gray diaper, even though he was four years old, old enough to open a jar and eat more than his share, but not old enough to use the toilet. "Tommy, darn it! Nobody's going to want to eat that now you've stuck your whole hand in it. Give me that."

I grabbed the jar but it was greasy and he hung on tight with two hands, hollering until it slipped from his grasp. One hand went immediately into his mouth all the way up to the wrist. The other grabbed the hem of Mother's housedress I was wearing and tugged, trying to wrap it around his face. Tommy couldn't stand to have his hands free and not be pulling on something or sucking his fingers; he acted like he might fall over if he didn't hang on tight. His face was smeared with peanut butter and snot. It was even in his hair. He started to cry.

"Stop it." I yanked my dress free. He looked startled and his crying changed to big hiccups. I picked him up, balanced him on my hip, and reached for the last green sucker in the jar on the counter. "Tommy, quiet. I've got to call Saint Maighread."

I had checked the calendar; it was September 2, 1963. I thought that school started in the morning, but I wasn't certain; we had to be there and on time. I also needed to find out about the used uniform sale. It didn't matter what we wore on the first day of school if it didn't smell or look dirty, but after that we needed to wear our uniforms: plaid jumpers, cardigan sweaters, white shirts, knee socks and saddle shoes for the girls; salt and pepper corduroys, white shirts and navy V-neck sweaters for the boys. Margaret, who was six, could wear my old uniform. David still fit into his from last year. He was thirteen and seemed to have stopped growing; I was only eleven, but I had grown so much over the summer that I fit into Mother's clothes. I stuck the candy in Tommy's mouth and while he gulped down his sobs with hungry slurps of green sugar, I looked up the number for school and dialed.

I balanced the receiver on my shoulder. "This is Rose Concannon," I said. I kissed Tommy's sticky cheek and set him down on the floor, but he started to whimper again. I surrendered and handed him my skirt hem to fist and suck with his candy so he wouldn't make too much noise while I was talking to Sister Mary Francis.

"Yes, S'ter. No, S'ter. Yes, S'ter. We'll be there. No, we plan to be on time, yes S'ter, every day. Yes, S'ter, we have an alarm clock. Everything's fine, as fine as can be. I was just calling to check who's teaching first grade so I can tell Margaret. Yes, S'ter. Mother? Much better. Fine, she's fine. She's perfect."

2

MISS MURPHY

Q: What are the sins against hope?
A: The sins against hope are presumption and despair.

Baltimore Catechism: The Truths of Our Catholic Faith

This year I hoped to get us to school every day, clean and on time with our homework completed. Margaret's hair needed braiding and her underwear couldn't smell like urine. David needed to dig the dirt from under his fingernails and scrub his neck. I needed to stop tapping my fingers and jiggling my legs. If the nuns noticed us, things could get dangerous again.

Last year when the Catholic Aid Society lady came to "assess our situation," I thought she had come to help. I thought things were going to get better. Before she took

Lucille she talked to each of us. She asked us what we needed. David was an idiot. He said he wanted the entire set of *The Books of Knowledge*, like this was Christmas and the Aid Society lady was Santa Claus. I told her we needed baby bottles and formula and clean diapers for Tommy and Lucille and washing machine detergent and something for little Lucille's hot red diaper rash. I told her we needed toilet paper and milk. I told her Tommy's nose was running all the time and how he never listened to anything anyone ever said, even my father. I left out the things that would make Mother look bad.

The lady I told these things to sat in our best chair while she listened to me. I had put a towel on the cushion before she sat down because Tommy had peed on it. She smoothed the back of her suit skirt as she sat down, and when she folded her legs her nylons swished. I couldn't take my eyes off her shiny, pointy-toed shoes. She was the prettiest lady I had ever seen, and she was listening to everything I said and nodding and writing it all down on her clipboard. I wanted to tell her enough to keep her interested but not enough to scare her away. Before she left she told me that if I needed anything, anything at all, to let her know. She would be back.

I had decided to ask for something for myself—I would ask for a hairbrush—but when she came again a week later with another lady just like herself, she handed me a jar of colored suckers. I could see that she wasn't here to talk this time. The two of them just clickety-clacked around the house in their high-heeled church shoes looking at everything. They even looked in the bathroom. Then they went into my mother's room and lifted Lucille right out of her crib and carried her away without asking permission from my mother, who was sitting right there watching it all happen.

My father was home then, too. He sat at the kitchen table with his hands folded in front of him like a naughty child saying his Act of Contrition while those two ladies marched right past him carrying Lucille.

Lucille was smiling her toothless smile as she disappeared out the door. The first lady, who wasn't carrying Lucille, stopped and spoke to my father. "Mister Concannon, we'll be back next week to check on you and we'll have some papers. God bless you. Thank you for your cooperation. You did the right thing. My name is Miss Murphy. Good bye, Rose."

She set a neat white card on the table in front of his thumbs. I watched to make sure it stayed there so I could dial the number later and tell them I'm a good girl, I take real good care of Lucille and my mother. We just ran out of a few things that one time you were here. So you don't need to worry, just bring Lucille back home, because I'm sure she must be lost without me.

Later that day I mopped the kitchen floor with ammonia and stacked the entire collection of empty cans out on the back porch so when they came again they would see that we were managing and they would bring me back my Lucille.

Lucille never did come back and I didn't know where she was. Nobody would tell me. Every time I phoned, Miss Murphy talked to me in the nicest voice I had ever heard in my entire life and I wondered why since she had already taken what she wanted.

She said that Lucille was safe and happy and not to worry about her, but it wasn't Lucille I was worried about. I knew ladies like them would keep her clean and fat.

Didn't I tell them it was me who changed her diapers and rocked her to sleep with a warm bottle all those times, sniffing and nuzzling the top of her fuzzy head, soft as a pussy willow, while she sucked and stared into my eyes?

3

WE WENT TO THE BEACH

Q: What are we commanded by the seventh commandment?
A: By the seventh commandment we are commanded to respect what belongs to others. We must not cheat. This means we may not copy answers from someone else in the classroom.

Baltimore Catechism: The Truths of Our Catholic Faith

Mother and the new baby were still asleep and safe in the middle of the wide bed. Mother had left several wet diapers in a pile in the corner of the floor and the baby wore a fresh dry one fastened with little yellow duck safety pins. Mother was a good mother when she was able.

I peeked inside the diaper and saw that this baby was a girl. Elise is what I named her. "Elise," I said. I pressed my face into her soft tummy. Her skin smelled like Mother's: lemon, salt, and rain, and her own baby smell like clean, new fruit. I licked her soft tummy. Mother would take good care of her new baby, but I wondered what to do about Tommy. He couldn't get into too much trouble if I locked him in his bedroom with the peanut butter, a can of black olives (his favorite), and some pans and spoons to bang on.

David and Margaret were awake. I poured them some Trix and milk into bowls and told them to hurry up and get dressed. And brush your teeth, I reminded them. It didn't matter what we wore on the first day as long as it didn't smell.

On the first day of school the teacher liked to ask personal questions. Father had told me not to tell our business to anyone, so I never knew what to say. In the classroom we always sat alphabetically, which put me near the front, behind the twins, Fiona and Patrick Brown. After we answered how many brothers and sisters we had and how we spent our summer vacations, the nuns would smile for the first and last time and say something like: There, now I know all about you, Class. This sounded like a lie to me. I didn't have friends, but I knew that it took more than one conversation.

Last year after Patrick Brown told about visiting his cousins in Monroe and almost drowning in a river, I rose and stood beside my desk, as I was supposed to, but I could think of absolutely nothing to say. Sister Olivia, who didn't know me yet, was patient. "Miss Concannon?" I was silent. "Miss Concannon? What did you do this summer?"

"Nothing, S'ter."

"That is impossible. You must have done something." The other children stared at their desks, not listening, thinking about when it would be their turn to lie about their own crummy vacations. "Miss Concannon? We are waiting."

I couldn't think of a single thing that was anything like what I knew she wanted to hear, but I had to say something before I could sit down again, so I told the truth. I told her I was busy trying to teach my brother, Tommy, to poop in the pot because he was getting too big for me to chase all over the house and sometimes into the alley, trying to change his diapers on the run. This got everyone's attention and they laughed, except Sister, who adjusted her veil and wimple. "Miss Concannon, that is quite inappropriate."

"Yes, S'ter, it is," I said. "He's three years old and I'll be darned if I want to change messy diapers that size for much longer."

I spent the remainder of the day in Sister Superior's office while she and the nurse, Sister Mikey, took turns asking me questions. Tell us about your mother. Tell us about your "domestic situation." What do you eat for breakfast? Do you have any questions?

Yes, how do you get a great big over-sized brother to eat with a spoon instead of his hand? And how do I keep fried eggs from sticking to the pan so I don't waste half? And why can't my mother stay home for the rest of her life? I take good care of her. But these things were just what I was thinking. What I said was: No, S'ter.

They didn't ask anything about my father, which was too bad. They would have been relieved to hear that he had a good job again, working for Boeing in Everett, only forty miles north of Seattle, and we saw him almost every weekend, but I had been reminded many times by my teachers to "Answer only the question you are being asked, Miss Concannon."

The next day Sister Mikey, Mother Superior, and two ladies, who later took Lucille, talked to me. I swear on the holy rosary, I didn't know they were planning to take Lucille or I would have lied. I would have told them we went to the zoo and the movies for our family vacation.

I have prayed every night to the Virgin Mary for forgiveness. *Holy Mary, Mother of God, pray for us sinners.*

I have a new teacher this year, Sister Norbert, and when she calls on me, I won't say that Tommy still isn't potty-trained a whole year later. No, I will remember what Bridget O'Faolain, who is perfect, said she did on her vacation last year. She and her whole family, even her cousins, went to the ocean beach and played chase with the waves. They rented ponies and bought tickets for the Ferris wheel. That is what I will say I did this summer. Bridget O'Faolain is exactly what the nuns want, so I will watch her all the time and be like her.

When Sister Norbert finally got to the part of the day where she asked about our summers, I was prepared, but while other students told their lies, I couldn't listen. I was worrying about the new baby girl, Elise, and Tommy. I hoped Mother would feel well enough to change her diaper so she wouldn't get a burning red rash and I hoped Tommy could last the whole day in his room and not cry so loud he would disturb Mother and the neighbors would hear. I decided to sneak home at lunchtime and check on them. "I can't think about them now," I whispered.

Sister scowled. "Miss Concannon, you must wait your turn to speak." I tried to remember to concentrate. I watched Bridget closely. If I did everything she did, if I crossed my ankles and folded my hands on my desk, if I made sure my sharp pencil stayed in the little groove on my desk and not on the floor, maybe no one would notice I was shaking.

4

SINS AND SACRAMENTS

*Before you go to confession, examine your con-
science, and then look at a crucifix for at least a
minute to see what sin has done to Our Lord.*

*Baltimore Catechism: The Truths of Our
Catholic Faith*

Friday afternoon was our weekly confession time. We
had our heads down on our desks corralled in our
arms as we meditated on our sins in preparation for
Confession. After we had figured out our sins, we would
line up and walk next door to Saint Maighread Catholic
Church to make our confessions to Father O'Brien.

Sister Norbert had pulled the tall shades to keep out
the late October afternoon sun and to keep us from daydreaming. She was right about that. All the trees were

turning red and yellow. A person couldn't help but stare at the things that were getting better right before your eyes.

I tried to concentrate on what Sister was saying. "Boys and Girls, Confession is a sacrament and we are blessed to receive it. Only those baptized in the Roman Catholic Church may receive the blessings of this most holy sacrament. Jesus loves to forgive us. It gives Him His greatest joy." Sister swept up and down the aisles as she spoke, depositing a folded piece of paper on each desk. It said: "A Child's Meditation on Sin: A Checklist for Confession." We took out our pencils.

The room was silent except for the sloppy sniffles of Danny Barry wiping his snotty nose on the back of his hand, the clack of Sister's wooden rosary beads hanging from her waist, and the muffled sound of her rubber-soled shoes as she swept up and down the aisles, her heavy black habit and veil floating behind her. She stopped when she came to me.

Her firm hand squeezed my shoulder and she whispered in my ear: "Relax." Her breath was dry. I stopped rocking and stared at my desktop until she lifted her hand and moved on. I tried hard to be good, but my hands belonged to someone else and my fingers just kept going, patting and thumping like crazy. Finally I sat on them to stop the drumming.

She passed out the same pamphlet every Friday. I knew all the sins by heart, but I always read every word anyway. I didn't want to leave anything out.

Once Sister had asked what we wanted to be when we grew up. Bridget said she wanted to be a nun. Danny whispered, "Probably a saint. Maybe she'll get her picture on a holy card and we can get her autograph." I planned to be a sinner.

Confession was my favorite activity of the week. I liked deliberating how many times I had committed each sin and marking the number in the little box beside the sin. I liked planning the sins I would commit during the following week. I tried to rotate and not have the same confession each time. I had committed nearly every venial sin on the list, and some I had committed many times. Sometimes I would whisper the beautiful-sounding names of the worst sins—the mortal sins: adultery, false witness, sloth, and gluttony. I planned to commit every sin on the list before I died.

Bridget O'Faolain sat across the aisle from me, so close I could have leaned over and kissed her. She was tiny and perfect and only nine years old, two years younger than the rest of the class; she had been double promoted because she had memorized the entire Mass in Latin and she could figure out five digit long-division problems in her head when she was six. She skimmed her list quickly, sliding her slender finger down the page, and then she picked up a long sharp pencil and wrote a teensy number 2 next to "I disobeyed my father and mother." When she was done, she squinted at her work, and then carefully erased the number 2, blew the pink eraser crumbs from her page, and wrote a number 1. Then she covered her work under a blank sheet of paper, returned her pencil to the groove at the top of her desk, and rested her head back down on her arms. Her hair spread on her desk like a silk fan. I was tempted to lean over and blow on her hair to see it lift and settle again into the same perfect, shiny, crescent shape, but I resisted. Instead I licked my fingers and smoothed my frizzy bangs.

The church was hot and smelled of incense and spoiled lilies. As we filed in I pushed right up next to Bridget. She dipped her fingers into the Holy Water font and I dipped my fingers exactly where she had made a circling ripple. She crossed herself, fingertips to forehead, chest, left shoulder, and then right. I crossed myself, too, staying just one gesture behind her. *In the name of the Father and of the Son and the Holy Ghost, Amen.* She genuflected down on one knee and bowed her head and crossed herself again. I did the same and we rose together. I grinned at how matched we were but when I looked at Bridget to see if she was grinning, too, she flipped her black hair with her pale hand like she didn't care if we were the Siamese twins from Borneo. We slid into the creaky wooden pew to wait.

Bridget sat erect with her eyes straight ahead toward the altar where the flickering candles burned; reminding us that Christ was present. Her eyelashes were so long you couldn't tell if her eyes were closed or opened. I tugged on my own lashes and examined the few that stuck to my fingertips. Sister rapped the back of the pew with her knuckles, so I copycatted Bridget. I stared straight ahead with my eyes all squinty, half shut and half opened. I stared

without blinking at the life-sized
at his open bleeding heart and t
David had taught me that if you s
a long enough time His face wou
alive. Sometimes His hand ever
enough to make you feel holy, or
of the Devil.

his coffe
in the
Lu

The church was so stuffy I felt faint. Every Sunday at least one person keeled over during mass. Maybe they kept the furnace blasting because people feel more sorry for their sins when they can hardly breathe.

Danny Barry came out of the confessional and knelt for a long time in front of me, whispering his penance. *Our Father, Who art in Heaven.* He went on forever. He must have committed a lot of sins to be making such a long penance. He must have committed even more sins than me. I wondered what he had done. I was impressed. This boy was worth knowing. I decided to ask him later, if I could stand to talk to him. I would write a note. Maybe we could share some ideas.

It was so quiet I could hear the insides of the other kid's bodies. I could hear them swallowing their saliva and their stomachs gurgling. Somebody smelled like farts. When it gets this quiet I have to make noises to distract me from my evil thoughts. Sister told us that sometimes a wicked thought is a sin, the same as if you committed the thing.

I had plans for most of the sins except murder. The only person I could conceive of murdering would be my father. Lately I had been thinking of how I could poison

e with Drano or I could electrocute him when he's
bathtub. He shouldn't have let them walk away with
cille without saying a single word. He didn't even kiss
her goodbye.

I wished my brain had an on/off switch. Sometimes it helped to make noises. I started to click my tongue. Click-clock. Bridget O'Faolain looked at me but when I smiled at her, she looked back at the altar. I added a swishy sound with my tongue. Click- clock, thonk, swish.

Sister tapped me on the shoulder. It was my turn. I slipped into the dark confessional and knelt. The shutter behind the screen slid open and I could make out Father O'Brien's round profile. I crossed myself and began. *Bless me, Father, for I have sinned, it has been one week since my last Confession.*

5

THE SHELTER OF OUR DESKS, NOVEMBER 1963

A good shepherd tries to protect his sheep from danger—such as danger from wolves, danger from floods, from cliffs and other things that might take the life of a sheep. And if the sheep is caught in a dangerous place, the shepherd goes to rescue it. We are the sheep who have fallen into the danger of sin through our own fault.

Baltimore Catechism: The Truths of Our Catholic Faith

The November day had turned as dark as night, but in the classroom the hanging lamps cast a warm yellow glow. Sister's chalk tapped and scraped against the blackboard, now and then emitting a teeth-chilling screech. Only Bridget O'Faolain prepared for her grammar assignment. The rest of us watched the clock, anxious for the minute hand to mark twelve o'clock. Bridget opened her blue cloth binder, pried the rings open, removed one sheet of paper, snapped the rings shut, and put it away inside her desk. She checked her pencil tip, started to get up to sharpen it, looked at the clock, saw that it was one minute before noon, folded her hands on top of her clean white page, and waited.

As the minute hand on the large-faced school clock jumped to 12, the Wednesday noon whistle blasted and we scrambled to the small private shelters beneath our desks. I steepled my arms over my head, and bowed my forehead to my saddle shoes as we had been instructed by the National Defense Council filmstrip. I held my breath, trying not to inhale the wet dirt smell of the leather. Only Sister stayed erect, patrolling up and down the aisles, offering safety instructions and explanation. "Don't look at the windows," she reminded us in her soft Irish lilt. "An atom bomb is bright enough to melt your eyeballs." I noticed the dust around the hem of her shoe-length skirt as she passed my desk. "If this were a real Soviet nuclear attack," she continued, "the air raid siren we all just heard would signal you to head to the closest bomb shelter with your family." I needed to find out where that was. If it weren't too far I could probably carry Tommy and my mother could carry Elise, but I would have to link arms with Mother to show her where to go. David and

Margaret could carry our provisions. My father could go to the bomb shelter at his job.

Across the aisle from me, Danny Barry picked with his ruler at the gum wads stuck to the bottom of his desk. Sister's sturdy black oxfords, as small as my sister Margaret's, paused between us. One of her shoelaces was broken and knotted together. She coughed into her hand. Danny stopped.

"Who is making that noise?" she asked. Danny slid his ruler under his legs, but Sister did not move. "Class, you might take the opportunity to offer up this time for your burning ancestors in Purgatory."

Danny shrugged and then craned his neck, trying to look under her long black skirts. When he noticed me watching, he shook his head, no; he could not see any ankles. "Master Barry," Sister said, "if this drill is so difficult for you, please close your eyes and concentrate on the suffering of Our Lord. He hung on the cross for three hours and He, Master Barry, was stripped naked. You, on the other hand, Young Man, are being asked to endure a mere three minutes under your desk." She leaned down and her wooden rosary slapped against the side of Danny's desk. Sister grabbed her rosary, kissed the crucifix, and leaned in to Danny's surprised, freckled face. "Master Barry," she whispered, "we all have legs." Danny hunched deeper under his desk, grinning and blushing.

Sister resumed her patrol and her lecture. "Boys and Girls, the Russian Communists are atheists. They will ask you to give up your faith and deny Christ." Danny resumed working on the gum. When at last he had freed a wad, he looked at me and stuck it in his mouth.

Danny Barry had once asked Sister how you could know if it was a real Russian air raid or not. She said that we could be certain this was merely a practice drill because it always sounded on Wednesday at exactly 12:00 noon. Danny had persisted, "What if the Red Commies are really smart and that's when they attack us, on a Wednesday at noon. How will we know if it's real or fake then?"

"Master Barry," she had said. "If you spent as much time thinking about your catechism drills as you do this other malarkey, you would be the smartest boy in this class."

I wanted to smile at Danny, but I was embarrassed and shy, wondering if he had read my note yet. What sins did you do, it said. And: Let's talk.

Bridget O'Faolain no longer sat across from me. Sister had made her trade places with Danny, who sat in the back, because, Sister said, he was much more interested in daydreaming out the window than in studying his grammar lessons. Maybe this was true, but I was still heading my paper and Danny had already finished his diagrams and was scrawling a note on a corner he had torn from his smudgy rumpled paper. He put down his pencil, folded the note into a parcel smaller than my fingertip, kissed it, and threw it onto my desk. I didn't want his note, but I didn't want him to get in trouble with Sister, so I stuck it in my cardigan pocket and glared at him.

Sister swooped down on me. "Miss Concannon," she said, "we have all had our fun and distraction for today," she meant the air raid drill, "and now it is time to do what?"

"Sentences," I whispered. On the blackboard Sister had written ten sentences in her tidy cursive script for us to copy and diagram. I continued heading my paper: name; subject—Grammar; and the date. I skipped a line, numbered the first sentence, and began to copy: God made us to…

"Rose Concannon, what have you forgotten?"

I checked the date. I had written: November 20, 1963. It matched the board. I shrugged. "I don't know, S'ter."

Sister tapped the top center of my page. "Your offering." JMJ, I wrote in my most beautiful loopy cursive: Jesus, Mary, Joseph. Sister nodded and continued her rounds. I lowered my shoulders and exhaled.

After school I opened Danny's smudgy crumpled note in the bathroom stall. The note looked a mess. He had drawn a big heart, erased once, and redrawn. Inside the heart he had written the initials: D.M.+ R.C. And beneath that he had scrawled: Go with me.

I dropped it in the toilet and flushed.

Danny found me on my way home. His sweater was caught in his jacket zipper, his shoes were untied, and he had grass stains on the knees of his salt-and-pepper cords.

"Did you read it?" he asked. His cheeks were red and his eyes were blue.

"You lost your hat," I said. I reached over and patted his hair.

"Yikes. Wait for me," he said. He dropped his lunch pail at my feet, which sprang open, and ran back, down the hill.

I picked up his lunch box and looked through the remains: an untouched banana, part of a bologna and mustard sandwich—which I stuck in my mouth, a rubber band, a bubblegum comic, some wadded-up wax paper, and the mother lode—a note—which I promptly read: I love you, Danny. Be a good boy. Study hard in school today. Love, Grandma. This did not sound like the correspondence of a fellow sinner. I stuck this in my coat pocket and stuffed everything else back in his lunchbox and snapped it shut.

He retrieved his hat and was running up the hill. "Thanks," he said, pulling the blue stocking-hat down over his big stick-out ears. "My grandmother knit this for me." I handed him his lunchbox.

"Did you read my note?" he asked. I fingered the other, stolen note in my pocket.

"Well," he said, "what do you think? Want to go with me? We don't have to hold hands or anything. Maybe just walk home together."

I rolled his grandmother's good-boy note into a hard little pea-sized ball and threw it at him. "Grandma's baby," I said. "You can go to hell."

I crossed the street and ran home.

6

A MOTHER'S COOKING

When we obey our parents we are obeying God. They have taken God's place. Besides obeying our parents in all that is not sinful, we must also help them. When we are helpful to our parents we can be sure that God is pleased.

Baltimore Catechism: The Truths of Our Catholic Faith

November 22, 1963, started out as the best morning of my life. I woke to the aroma of bacon and pancakes. This had never happened before, but I knew what I was smelling. I pulled on my clothes and stuck clips in my hair without combing it or even looking in the mirror. Then I pulled off Margaret's covers.

"Wake up. Mother's cooking."

She strained to open her eyes and asked sleepily, "What do you mean?"

I hurried down the hall to wake David, and then practically stumbled down the stairs, panicked that if I didn't get to the kitchen in time there would be none left.

Mother stood in front of the yellow stove holding a spatula in her hand, flipping pancakes. She was dressed in the cleanest clothes you have ever seen: blue denim dungarees rolled up to her knees and a bright yellow sweater, her hair pulled back with a blue-checkered ribbon. She looked as pretty and as real as T.V. The only thing missing was a pair of high-heeled shoes. Mother was barefoot.

"Mother," I said, "it's cold. I'll get your slippers." She looked at me and, this next part is true I swear, she asked me if I wanted one pancake or two. I wanted pancakes, but more than that I wanted to run to her and squeeze her with all the strength of my beating heart. I didn't though. She might vanish like a soap bubble if I even breathed too hard, so I sat in a chair at our kitchen table and waited for my very own mother to serve me breakfast.

She floated to the table with a plate of pancakes and bacon in one hand and a tall glass of brown liquid in the other.

"Have you ever had chocolate Ovaltine?" she asked. I hadn't.

Elise was belted into a cloth chair right in the middle of the table. She was flexing her toes and gumming a baby biscuit, the happiest baby God ever made, and Tommy was in his usual place under the table, scooping big handfuls of Cheerios and milk into his mouth, but he was dressed. He had on brown corduroy overalls, a matched striped shirt, and one sock. Mother picked up the stray sock that was nearby and slipped it on his foot.

Next David and Margaret came in. Margaret shot me a confused look that seemed to ask, "Should I be worried?" My mouth was full of warm, buttery, maple-flavored pancakes, so I just pulled out the chair next to me, patted the seat, and mumbled something that was meant to say, "Sit down." She sat and folded her hands in front of her on the table the way you do in school when you don't want Sister to call your name.

"Holy smokes! Have I entered a new dimension?" David said, but he was smiling. He scrambled into a chair, looked at Mother, and said, "Gee whiz, Mom, this sure looks swell," in a voice I had heard before somewhere, but not in this house. "There is nothing wrong with your T.V set," he said. He had entered a strange country and was testing out the local customs, but before he could say, "Do not adjust the horizontal," Mother set a stack of pancakes and a glass of Ovaltine in front of him. He took a sip, raised the glass as if offering a toast, and said, "It tastes good and is good for you, too." He looked at me for approval, but I wasn't going to play. This was real.

Margaret was madly swinging her leg under the table and picking at her pancakes with her fork. When uncooked batter oozed out of the center, she stuck her tongue out and looked to me for help. I shook my head, no, eat them, they're good.

"Mm," I mumbled. Margaret folded her gooey pancake and offered it to her feral brother under the table.

Mother noticed Margaret's empty plate immediately. "Done already?" she said, flipping another pancake onto her plate. As soon as Mother wasn't looking, David reached across the table and forked it into his mouth.

My father came in, smelling like soap, with a little blob of white shaving cream near his ear, which my mother reached out and removed with her little finger. Then she straightened the collar of his red flannel shirt, handed him his lunchbox, and kissed him on the cheek. David looked at me and raised his eyebrows and whispered, "Do you believe me now? This is Weirdsville," but he was wrong. When my father kissed her back my mother did not turn into a two-headed monster, she smiled and asked, "Will you be home for dinner, dear?"

After he had gone, David continued shoveling food into his mouth until his cheeks bulged like a chimpanzee's, his imitation of a hungry boy, all the while humming the theme from The Twilight Zone: doo doo doodoo, doo doo doodoo.

Mother was home, dressed, and cooking breakfast, just like I had always imagined she could, and everyone was acting so wrong, wrecking it. Margaret was scared to taste her breakfast. David was too awkward and stupid to be anything other than a smart aleck. Why couldn't my family just accept it? This is what it looks like. This is how it smells. This is how it tastes. This is what Happy is.

I threw my fork down and went to get my books. Mother didn't notice my annoyance. "Don't forget to brush your teeth before you go," she said.

"Aw, Ma," David said, still in character.

Margaret followed me up the stairs. "Do I have a toothbrush?" she asked.

On the way to school, David stopped.

"Hold everything." He popped open his lunchbox and laughed malevolently. "Ah ha!" he said with the delight of a mad scientist whose hypothesis has proved correct. He pulled a handful of unwrapped, dripping pancakes from his lunchbox. "You can take the girl out of the country," he said.

"Shut up," I said. "Can't you just let yourself enjoy some breakfast?" I grabbed Margaret's hand and crossed the street.

7

NOVEMBER 22, 1963

Q: What is a mystery?
A: A mystery is something we do not fully under-
stand, but which we firmly believe because it was
taught to us by Holy Mother Church.

Baltimore Catechism: The Truths of Our
Catholic Faith

Sister turned off the overhead lights and flicked on the single bright bulb of the filmstrip projector, which she had set up on a desk. The little motor whirred; she uncapped the lens and the white screen in the front of the room glowed. Immediately small eager shadows of bird-hands flew across the screen, chased by snapping silhouettes of sharks and dogs. A few squeals punctuated the birds' ascent as they fled their predators, and Sister scolded, "Boys and Girls, idle hands mean an idle mind."

After this, a lone Indian Chief popped up, wiggled his feathers, bowed, and the shadow theater ceased, then a graphic of crosshairs appeared on the screen and the word: Focus. Sister clicked the filmstrip forward past a series of frames of the word: Start. Finally, a red-hued photo of a large ship approaching New York Harbor filled the screen. "The Harbor," Sister read. The machine beeped and Sister clicked to the next frame. A red-hued, wide-angle view of a harbor with ships and boats of various sizes coming and going filled the screen. Sister read the white subtitles projected across the bottom of the image: "A harbor is more than just a refuge for ships." Beep. Click. "If the ship is from a foreign port, a doctor from The Quarantine Service also comes aboard." Beep. Click. "If there is evidence of a contagious disease, he examines all passengers." This frame revealed a smiling, dark-eyed mother holding her thin, bare-chested son as a bald, middle-aged man in a suit extended his stethoscope to the child's chest. Two bare-chested siblings, a boy and a girl, looked on, waiting their turn. Beep. Click. "Custom service men inspect for items that are taxable or against the law." Beep. Click. Sister crossed in front of the beam of light, and her arrow-shaped figure was momentarily overlaid between the images of two men in gas masks fumigating a ship. The class laughed. Someone said, "Look S'ter, you're with those guys." Sister moved out of the light and frowned, a silent warning to us to stay quiet.

We had been studying travel and transportation for two long weeks. So far we had been forced to endure filmstrips about cars, trailers, trains, airplanes, public transportation systems—buses, taxis, and subways—and private methods. Today, following the filmstrip, our project presentations began. I was trying different strategies to keep me awake. Drawing was never permitted, so I tried squeezing my eyes shut, wide-open, and shut again, until Sister waggled her finger at me.

Mary Theresa Mahoney had volunteered to present her project first, and as she droned on and on about the variety of personal transportation options we had in our modern democratic country compared to the limited options of less civilized countries like China, I pinched my thighs, hoping the quick sharp pain might defeat the drowsiness. "In some countries people even ride their bicycles to work," Mary Theresa explained.

This was nearly unbearable. I tried praying. Dear Blessed Virgin Mary, please, please; please don't let me fall asleep in class. I will get in so much trouble. Danny Barry was busy carving into his desktop with an opened paper clip. I tried to see what he was writing, but his elbows blocked my view. "So now you see," Mary Theresa was still talking, "personal transportation methods vary the world round and," she paused, made bold eye contact with her audience, then delivered the punch line, "just give thanks that you don't have to ride a donkey to school." Laughter and, praise God, she was finally done. She started to go to her desk then stopped, remembering something. No no no, no more, please. "Any questions?" she asked.

Danny's hand shot up.

"Yes, Danny Barry," Mary Theresa said, looking delighted that someone had taken enough interest to ask a question.

"Mary Theresa," he said, "no offense, but were you really interested in all that stuff?"

"Master Barry!" Sister said. "That was a very fine report, Mary Theresa." She scowled at Danny. "Now, Master Barry, since you are so interested, would you please present next?"

Danny Barry reached in his desk and as he pulled out his report, crumpled wads of paper and a comic book fell to the floor. He picked his things up and crammed them back in his desk.

"Master Barry, are you not ready?"

"Yes, S'ter. I mean no, S'ter." He ran to the front of the class. "Yes, S'ter."

"Which is it, Master Barry?" The class giggled.

"Ready, S'ter." He looked at the class and smiled shyly.

"Master Barry," Sister said, "tuck in your shirt before you begin." Danny tucked in his shirt, then held his report directly in front of his face and mumbled something.

"Master Barry. Let us see your cherubic face, please." Danny lowered his folder. His face was flushed. He grinned and grinned and then he started to giggle.

"Master Barry, when you have composed yourself, you may begin."

"Time..." Danny was giggling and could barely get his words out. I checked the clock—10:45—hoping this was the last report before recess. Danny cleared his throat, composed himself, and began again. "Time travel," he said.

I snapped awake.

"Imagine," he said, "if you could climb in a machine, turn a dial, and go all the way back to the time of Adam and Eve." A few drowsy heads lifted. Then, someone spoke: "Cool." Sister glared over her steel-framed spectacles at the class. "Boys and Girls," she hissed, but the word had been spoken and it floated like a ray of warm sun. Danny smiled and started to relax.

"Man has always imagined what it might be like to live in another time," he continued. "And physicists have even tried to build machines to make this possible." He grinned at us and then looked over his shoulder at Sister Norbert. She nodded, a sign of encouragement.

"I'll show you what one could look like." He reached in his back pocket and pulled out a piece of paper, unfolded it, and held up a crayon drawing of a boy seated in something that looked like a phone booth. He was wearing a helmet and his hands were adjusting some knobs. Danny pointed at the knobs. "This is the control panel," he said. "You can choose what time period you want to go to."

Someone whispered, "I would go to World War Two and blow up Japs." Sister looked up again and furrowed her brow.

Danny handed the picture to Sister. "You can put this up, if you want, S'ter," he said. He had everyone's attention now, but he was interrupted when the classroom door opened and in marched Sister Superior. Danny paused and the rest of us stood in unison, as we did when any adult entered the room.

"Good morning, Sister Superior," we said. She ignored us and strode to Sister Norbert's desk at the front of the class, adjusting her wimple and veil as if she had just slipped it on, while we stood beside our desks, waiting for her greeting and directive to be seated. She leaned toward Sister Norbert and whispered something in her ear. Sister Norbert jerked her head up and looked into Sister Superior's face. Sister Superior said something else, and then she nodded. Sister Norbert didn't say anything. Sister Superior then placed her hand on Sister Norbert's shoulder, a kind of intimate gesture that we had never seen between nuns before, and quickly left the room.

We waited, thinking someone must be in trouble. Danny Barry tucked in his chin, trying to hide in plain sight, the vanishing posture of boys who are scolded often. Sister didn't look at him. Instead she took her glasses from her face and lowered her head. I hoped it wasn't me who was in trouble. We continued to stand, waiting for instructions. Sister pulled a white handkerchief from inside her long black sleeve and wiped her glasses. A small tear slid down her cheek. Danny lifted his chin, realizing he was not the focus here, and looked over at her, then down at his paper, and then over at Sister again, and finally he whispered in his husky voice, "Sister?"

Sister replaced her glasses on her face, then looked up and stared at us, as if we were Martians. We were still standing at attention. "You may be seated, Class," she said.

Danny was still waiting to finish presenting his report. "Sister," he said, "do I continue?"

Sister Norbert looked at him. "No, Danny." She had called him by his first name. What was happening? "You may take your seat." Then she looked at us again. We sat with folded hands, thirty little saints, waiting to hear who was getting in trouble. My fingers started drumming on my desk.

"Boys and Girls." She stared at some invisible point at the back of the room, while we held our breath, waiting through a long silence. I stopped drumming my fingers. She removed her glasses again. A tear slid from her eye and pooled by the side of her nose. "Boys and Girls."

The class was restless now. Billy Winihan turned around and pointed at Tommy McGill. "I told you you're going to get it," he whispered. Sister ignored this, which was unprecedented.

"Boys and Girls," she finally said again. I noticed that without her glasses she had pale blue eyes. A thin strand of red hair had escaped from the tight wimple that circled her face. "Boys and Girls, I have just received some terrible news. It seems our president, our President Kennedy, has been shot." She spoke in a clear, thin voice. "We do not know the extent of his injuries." She reached her hand to

her face and tucked the red hair back into her wimple. "I
don't have any other news," she said. "I will be right back."
She nearly ran to the door, but she stopped before exit-
ing. "Miss Concannon," she said, "will you please come to
the front and lead the class in a prayer for our president's
recovery?"

"What prayer?" I asked.

"Hail Mary," Sister said as she hurried out the door.

I began my long walk to the front of the classroom.
"Please kneel," I said, as I knelt.

"In the name of the Father and of the Son and of the
Holy Ghost, Amen." I wiped my runny nose on my sweater
sleeve. "The Hail Mary," I said. "Hail Mary, full of grace,
the Lord is with thee."

We finished the prayer. Everyone sat in silence.

When Sister returned, her veil was crooked and she no
longer had her glasses. "Boys and Girls." She was fingering her rosary beads. I looked at the clock. Eleven twenty.
"Boys and Girls." She was speaking softly and slowly, one
word at a time. "Our dear Catholic president has been
shot. God bless his soul. There is no more school today.
You are dismissed." Sister then left the room.

No one moved. No one said a word. No one knew what
to do. We were used to lining up and waiting to be told
when to leave. Finally Danny stood and whispered like a
ventriloquist, without moving his lips, as if Sister were still
present. "Let's go."

I grabbed my coat and followed him to the door. He
tugged his stocking hat from his pocket and pulled it over

his big stick-out ears. His eyes were watering. "I would have had an A," he said.

I reached over and yanked his hat down over his eyes. "A+," I said.

8

MOURNING

Q: What does the fifth commandment forbid?
A: The fifth commandment forbids murder, and
suicide, and also fighting, anger, hatred, drunk-
enness, reckless driving and bad example.

Baltimore Catechism: The Truths of Our
Catholic Faith

W hen we got home from school the house was quiet. Mother was nowhere to be seen. A broken jam jar was scattered all over the kitchen floor and there was Tommy, sitting in the middle of it scooping red goop into his mouth and rocking back and forth like a retard, making appreciative grunts.

I yelled at him, "Jesus, Tommy," but he didn't even look up, and when I picked him up he howled and kicked and tried to escape. I hung on tightly, even though he was as heavy as a sack of stones, and I said a silent Hail Mary as I lugged him to the next room to deposit him in front of the T.V even though I knew he wouldn't stay. He was the only kid I knew who didn't even notice when the T.V. was on, even if you sat him right in front of it. I knew it was a sin that I was more concerned how he had stunk up my school uniform with pee than I was about the possibility of him swallowing glass. Anyway, he was such a tough little kid I knew it couldn't really hurt him.

Mother no longer resembled even the shadow of the mother in the bright yellow sweater who had been flipping pancakes in the kitchen several hours ago. She was sitting on the sofa, dressed in my father's green terrycloth bathrobe, sobbing as she watched the Kennedy motorcade on T.V. Jackie Kennedy was young and smiling in a pink suit and a matching pert little hat. Her husband, the president, was waving and smiling, looking as cool and handsome as a movie star. The sun was shining and people were waving their flags and signs and holding up their babies. Suddenly the president jerked forward, then jerked toward Jackie and something sprayed all over her, his brains. Jackie leaned toward him and her mouth was a wide O. Screaming, surprised? Next she was scrambling over the back of the car trying to get away, trying to save her own life, and a man in a suit was running with long strides to catch the limousine and he was climbing onto the back and reaching out to Jackie and trying to push her back in as the car was speeding away.

"Look at that," Mother said. "See how her hat stays on her head."

I set Tommy down next to Mother and he started to run back to the kitchen. "Stay there!" I said, but he kept running, so I grabbed him from behind, sat him on the sofa, and said right into his face with the fiercest look I could manage, "Stay! I will get you food later. Mother, hold onto him. Mother, where is Elise?"

Mother didn't answer. "Mother, listen to me. Where is Elise? Is she napping? Do I need to feed her?"

Mother finally looked at me and smiled. "The little girl?" she asked in a sweet voice. "I was giving her a bath. She must be clean now."

Mother had forgotten Elise in her little plastic tub that sits in the middle of the big bathtub. She was lying in about two inches of cool water; blue with cold, but alive and alert enough to fret and raise her arms the minute I said her name. The radio beside the tub was still on.

Elise, Elise. I wrapped her in a towel and held her tight against my chest and carried her to the living room.

"Mother! You left the baby in the bath!"

Mother was staring at the motorcade again.

"Mother, please. Listen to me. Take Elise. Hold on to her."

She looked at me and smiled sweetly. "Oh. Yes. The little baby girl." She smiled at Elise, a smile as bright as anybody's mother, and stretched out her arms.

"Are you all nice and clean?" she asked in the high-pitched voice mothers use with babies.

I handed Mother her baby.

"Rose," Mother said, "someone shot our handsome president."

"What's to eat?" Margaret asked.

I went to the kitchen to heat some Campbell's tomato soup.

We sat in front of the T.V. all afternoon watching the news coverage from Dallas and New York. We watched as Walter Cronkite read something on his desk, then removed his glasses, looked the nation in the eye, and announced, "From Dallas, Texas, the flash, appears official, President Kennedy died at one o'clock Central Standard Time." He cleared his throat and resumed. "Some thirty-eight minutes ago."

"Well, that's that," Mother said. "I guess the Protestants won't be converted after all."

David, who was standing in the doorway looking pale, smiled a wry smile and said, "Mother, Kennedy is the president, not a missionary."

As Cronkite continued with news about Lyndon Johnson, Mother got up and began wandering around the house as dazed as a sleepwalker, from the T.V. to the kitchen to the front door, which she kept opening and looking out. Maybe she was hoping my father would come home and make things better.

Her rapid decline since breakfast might have seemed more extreme had it not been that the whole world had changed so much on that November morning. Tommy was calm; maybe being positioned between Mother and me on the sofa was what held him. Elise, who had nearly drowned, was sitting on Margaret's lap looking very drowsy but fighting it. Her eyes kept closing and then snapping open. Maybe she didn't want to miss out on being with all of us together all at once; maybe she was afraid she'd be forgotten in the bathtub again. Margaret kept whispering to her over and over, "Don't worry, Baby, don't worry."

Only David seemed unchanged and he wouldn't stop talking. "If someone accidentally pushed the button and set off the nuclear missiles right now, before they swear in Johnson," he said, "there would be no one to answer the hotline. This might be the beginning of the end of the world, as we know it," he said. "We're probably closer to nuclear extinction than we were when Kennedy almost got us blown off the map over Cuba."

Mrs. Kennedy was walking up some stairs onto a plane. She looked like she was the last person left on the earth, even though several steps behind her there was another woman, dressed just like her, but not pretty. Her friend? Her secretary? Mrs. Johnson? Mrs. Kennedy looked straight ahead and walked up and up, one step, two steps, three steps; she was no longer wearing her hat, but she was still wearing the pink suit. And she was still wearing gloves.

"Always a lady," Mother's voice was full of admiration. She was crying and I was crying and David was laughing softly and shaking his head and Mrs. Kennedy was still climbing the stairs and all the while the voice of an unseen man was telling us that Mrs. Kennedy was ascending the stairs of the plane.

"Would you look at that? It's a miracle that she can remember how to climb up the stairs. All alone. All the way to the very top," my mother said. "Look at her. Right foot. Left foot." Mother shook her head and did she laugh or was she crying? "Holy God," she said. "If there was ever a time a woman needed to be carried."

Throughout the day David's commentary continued and eventually his voice became like a background sound, as inconsequential as the B-flat moan of the refrigerator, but it did not stop, even as we watched Lyndon Johnson, with one hand on the Bible and the other raised like a Boy Scout, being sworn in as president with Lady Bird on one side and Mrs. Kennedy on the other, still wearing the blood and brains of her young husband on her suit. She looked as stoic as a saint, not three hours since her husband's brains had exploded all over her lap, and I knew I was watching the loneliest person in the world and I wondered how a person could endure this.

David was either blind or he was missing a heart, because he talked on and on and laughed from time to time and I wondered how could he care about anything besides poor Mrs. Kennedy right then? He would not stop and he had never needed an interested audience to keep him going. He was telling us, even though no one cared, how Sister Joseph Marie said the Commies were out to destroy Catholicism because they hated anyone who believed in Jesus. He said now he agreed with her and this was proof. The end of the world was coming.

The news said a suspected assassin had been apprehended and David laughed. "Don't be stupid," he said. "Catholics know the Chinese Commies are in on it. First they get Kennedy, next they'll probably go after Cardinal Spellman."

I didn't know if he was being sarcastic or not. "David!" I couldn't take it any more. "The only one who gives a damn about the stupid Catholics is the goddamn holy Pope of Rome. So shut up!"

My mother looked up, her eyes were wide. "Rose, we don't say shut up in this house."

David roared with laughter at this and slapped his leg. "We don't say shut up in this house? Right. Right, Mother. We don't. We don't say shut up. Not in this house. No sir-ree. In this house we can drown the baby in the bath tub, but we can't say shut up."

"Shut up," I said again, but Mother was no longer listening.

When I turned to David, to make sure he had heard me, he had his face buried in his hands and his laughter now sounded like sobs. "God damn it," he said. "God fucking damn it."

Mother had returned her attention to the T.V. where the presidential motorcade drove through the crowds, over and over again, and Mrs. Kennedy scrambled for her life, over and over again, and the Secret Service agent dashed onto the rear of the limousine again and again and you wanted to scream watching it because no one was stopping it, no matter how many times they tried. It was like a horror show where the victims are entering the empty house and they seem so stupid and vulnerable and you know what is coming, of course you do, because you have seen this so many times before, but even so, you can't warn them and you can't stop them. In between watching the motorcade, we watched the whole world crying. We watched a smartly dressed woman on the street in New York fall back into the crowd as she heard the news from the radio in a passing car. We watched men in hard hats crying at their worksites in Boston; we saw old Colored ladies in Atlanta wiping their tears with white handkerchiefs; we saw stunned diners sitting at a lunch counter in Los Angeles watching the news and crying. When they showed Mrs. Kennedy standing beside Lyndon Johnson in her blood-spattered suit for the tenth time, I remembered about the two little kids, John and Caroline, and wondered if they would miss their handsome father? I forgot the Campbell's tomato soup I had warming on the stove until I smelled it burning.

"And to think she still manages to look so pretty," my mother said.

9

OUR DEAR CATHOLIC PRESIDENT

*Jesus obeyed His parents on earth. He obeyed
Mary, His mother, and Joseph, His foster father.
He knew that His heavenly Father had given
them power, or authority over Him.*

*Baltimore Catechism: The Truths of Our
Catholic Faith*

Mother was cooking breakfast again, pancakes again, bacon again, Ovaltine again, and something new—orange juice. She was smiling and talking and singing as she worked. Elise was buckled in her seat on the table again and Margaret was breaking apart her pancakes again and stirring them into the syrup until they resembled dog food. Tommy was in his usual place under the table. David kept his eyes averted, and his face was as pale and gray as cold ashes.

Mother had bought a pink suit and a little pillbox hat, which she was wearing that morning while she cooked. She even wore gloves.

"Mother," I said. "That suit!"

She smiled, a smile that would have made a baby coo, if it weren't all so creepy.

"Marked down." Then, like a T.V. model on The Price Is Right, calling your attention to a shiny new car or a gleaming refrigerator— big enough to hold enough milk and cherry Jell-O for everyone—she swept her hands down the lines of the skirt.

"The Bon Marché." She spun once and then froze, her arm raised and bent coquettishly at the wrist. "Chanel. A copy, but who can tell? I picked it up for twenty-nine dollars. Can you believe it?"

"Unfortunately, yes." David's grin was frozen like that freckled kid on the peanut butter jar. "It looks so...help me, Rose...what is the word I am looking for? Oh, yes, psycho."

"Oh," Mother's voice dropped. She smoothed her jacket sleeves with the backs of her fingers, erasing his comment.

"It seemed so cheerful. Pink. You know, Jackie has one just like it."

David shoveled the last several bites of Margaret's smashed pancakes into his mouth until his cheeks bulged like Chip and Dale's.

"Got to go. Math test." He stormed out the door, but Mother hurried after him, waving like a beauty queen from her parade float.

"Have a nice day, dear."

I tried to peck Mother on the cheek but missed and kissed her nose. She laughed and handed me three empty lunch boxes. "All geniuses need their nutrition."

Margaret and I had to run to catch up to David, already disappearing around the corner.

"Those gloves," he said, when we caught up to him.

"Yeah, she really liked Jackie." I handed him his non-lunch.

He shook the empty tin box. "Yum." He looked like he wanted to cry. "Got a quarter?"

⁓

I was happy to get back to school. Everything was the same, except for the gold-framed photo of JFK that now hung in the front of the classroom beside the portraits of the Sacred Heart of Jesus, Pope John the XXIII, and the Immaculate Heart of Mary.

As we knelt and prayed our Morning Offering, Sister asked that we include a silent prayer for the family of our dear Catholic president. Danny Barry raised his hand.

"Master Barry?" Sister smiled patiently.

Danny jumped to his feet and shook his head, looking confused. "S'ter, no disrespect, but shouldn't we be praying *for* the president, too, and not just his family? In case he's in Purgatory?"

Sister pressed her crucifix to her lips. "Master Barry, what have I told you about this?"

Danny stood beside his desk, hands at his sides like a soldier, still smiling, but his eyes had darkened.

"Well, Master Barry?" Sister fingered her rope of black wooden rosary beads.

"Question less and pray more?" he asked.

Sister smiled and nodded. "Please be seated, Master Barry." Her hand swept toward the portrait of John Kennedy.

"Boys and Girls let me assure all of you, our dear martyred Catholic President is in Heaven. He no longer needs your prayers. Very soon you will probably be praying to him, not for him."

Danny waved his hand.

Sister glared at him, but her voice was soft. "Patience is a virtue," she said. "Yes, Master Barry?"

Danny jumped to his feet. "Sister!" His face looked Eddie Haskell–serious. "What will we pray to him for?"

Sister spoke very slowly. "All Catholics must pray that he may continue in Heaven the work he was unable to finish here on earth."

"Like stopping the red Russians from trying to turn Catholics into Atheists?" Danny asked. "And don't you need three miracles to be a saint?"

"Miss Monaghan," Sister said. "Will you please tell Master Barry what our president's greatest work was?"

Mary Ellen stood.

"Yes, Sister." She turned to Danny and smiled smugly. "President John Kennedy's most challenging and important work on earth was the conversion of America to Catholicism."

Danny whispered through his praying fingers, "My brother, Dennis, said Kennedy knew Marilyn Monroe. I wonder if he converted her?"

10

WALK HOME WITH ME

*Jesus is our King and Judge. Someday we will
appear before Jesus our King. He will judge us
and all we have ever done. But He will do it in
a simple way. He will look in our hearts to find
one thing—love.*

*Baltimore Catechism: The Truths of Our
Catholic Faith*

What I knew much later was this: Paris Georgina
Jones was the most beautiful human being I
had ever laid eyes on, but the first time I ever
saw her, I didn't realize she was the answer to my prayers.
She certainly didn't look like any kind of messenger from
God.

In January it had snowed and school was closed for
three days. When the snow began to melt and school

resumed, we trudged reluctantly through a gray slush that coated the grass and hills, wishing for something, anything, to delay our return, but we knew school was inevitable and the best we could hope for was monotony.

The yellow classroom lights buzzed and flickered and the heat was on too high. The windows were frosted over and opaque from our warm breath, so there was nowhere to look to daydream. As usual, I was struggling to stay awake. I dreaded falling behind and having to repeat sixth grade. My brother David was thirteen and in the seventh grade for the second time. He had told me the only reason he hadn't kept up with his work was because it was too boring. He told me that if he had been polite they probably would have made him skip a grade.

"They confuse manners with intelligence," he said. "So here I am. When I'm sixteen, I'm dropping out and getting on with my life."

My health book lay open on my desk and I was copying in my best cursive the three main reasons for washing your hands, when the classroom door swung open and in walked a new student. She had arrived alone. The already quiet room grew silent as the whole class held its breath and stared at the first Colored girl any of us had seen up close, but the new girl didn't seem to notice us. She came wiggle-waggle, wiggle-waggling up the aisle with her unbuckled, two-sizes-too-big galoshes flapping against her skinny legs and plopped herself into the only empty bench in the sixth grade, right in front of me. Sister stood, raised one eyebrow slightly, nodded, and smiled. She had been expecting her.

"Boys and Girls, we have a new student today." Sister put her hand on Paris's shoulder. "This is Paris Jones."

Sister had barely pronounced the s on Jones when Paris shrugged off her touch.

"Paris *Georgina* Jones," she said. "Paris Georgina Jones."

Paris wasted the entire morning trying to arrange her arms and legs and elbows and knees into her desk. She twisted and wriggled and once she bent over so far in her bench that all her skinny braids brushed the floor. I had never witnessed a person try so hard to fit into a desk and stay there. Compared to Paris Georgina Jones, I might as well have been a holy statue stuck up on an altar.

After lunch it looked like Paris had wriggled herself to death. She was sitting at her desk, quiet and still. I opened my math book and began to copy from a page on converting fractions, but just as I was converting 8/24ths into thirds, Paris leaned her head all the way over backwards onto my desk, so I could see up her nostrils, and stared at me. She smelled like warm oranges, and I was about to tell her this when she crossed her eyes at me. I tried not to laugh out loud, but I crossed my eyes back at her, thinking we were two friends having fun.

"You're ugly," she said. I picked up my pencil to let her know I could poke her in the eye, but then I heard a whisper from behind me. "There but for the grace of God go I." I turned to look at Bridget, all the way at the back of the classroom, copying math problems into her note-book, and I wondered if I had heard anything at all or had just read her mind. I stared long enough to see her finish with her math book, put it away, and take out something to read, the thing to do if you were finished early, which had never happened to me. By the time I turned around again Paris Georgina Jones had lost interest in me and was making puff-puff noises with her lips at Danny Barry, who ignored her.

I got a whole week behind in my schoolwork just from star-ing at Paris. At first I didn't know that I was liking her. When I woke up in the morning, instead of thinking about breakfast or worrying about math, I was imagining the bright sound of Paris's voice. She looked and walked like a feral cat, quick, but secret, and at the base of her scalp, she had a tiny red scab where she had scratched too much. I was afraid to look at her for too long because she didn't seem to like it, but I couldn't look away, either. Every time she shook her braids, colorful plastic beads clattered to-gether like tiny wind chimes.

One day Paris Georgina Jones turned around and caught me writing with spit on my desk: P.G.J.

"Are those my initials?"

"If you own the letter P, they are," I said.

"Yes, as a matter of fact, I do own the letter P. And G. and J., too." And then she stuck her own slender brown finger right into my spit and erased the letters to prove that she meant it.

"You better mind your own business," I whispered. "Besides, I don't even know or care what your initials are." Then I spit on my desk again and dipped my finger into the foamy puddle.

"You better not," she said, but she snapped her head back around to where it belonged as Sister swept down the aisle, fast and smooth, like she had gliders instead of feet under her long black habit. I slid my math book over the top of my spit writing and flipped it open. I fixed a look of wrinkled concentration on my forehead. Sister whispered something to Paris first, but by the time she turned to me, I looked very busy. I had completed one problem and was erasing another with the tip of my index finger.

"Tsk," Sister said. I kept working, pretending to be too absorbed to have noticed her. "Tsk," she said again. I looked into her face. The ceiling lights reflecting opaquely on her lenses made her look fierce.

I stuck my eraser finger in my mouth and sucked the bitter lead taste. There was a smudgy black hole in my paper where I had erased.

"Can someone please lend Miss Concannon an eraser?" Sister asked. Danny Barry grinned sympathetically at me. He knew Sister's words were code for a public announcement that my work was wrong and a mess.

"Sorry, S'ter," I said softly.

Sister floated to the door, turned for a long moment, and studied the class; then nodded to Bridget O'Faolain, raised her eyebrows once, meaningfully, and left the room. Bridget brought her book and pencil to Sister's desk where she would sit, in charge of the class, until Sister returned. This was Paris's chance to do something that she had wanted to do since she arrived. She got down on her hands and knees and crawled up and down the aisles, inspecting the undersides and contents of all the desks in the class, which was something I, too, had wondered about. After crawling around the entire room and craning her neck under each and every desk, she returned to her own bench and turned to face me. Her face was glowing. She cupped her hand over her mouth so nobody else would hear the secret.

"Nancy's got gum all stuck up under her desk, but I don't think she's the one who chewed it. That skinny boy, Billy, he's got gum, too, a big pink gob of it. He probably chewed it today. Everybody's got boogers."

"Gross," I said, but this made me start to giggle, which I had never done with another child before.

Paris's eyes flashed, pleased that she had made me laugh.

"Bridget, she's the only one with no boogers. That girl probably doesn't have any in her nose, neither. The inside of her desk is clean, too. It looks like nobody sits there." I held my nose to keep from laughing.

When Paris grinned, her straight white teeth sparkled between her fingers.

"Walk home with me," I said.

11

VALENTINE'S DAY

*When we obey we are listening to the voice of
Our Good Shepherd. We are showing how much
we love Him. We do this especially when we obey
in something we do not feel like doing.*

*Baltimore Catechism: The Truths of Our
Catholic Faith*

On Valentine's Day my father decided to talk to us. He had news, he said, great news, he said, important news.

He called us all to the table like this:

Allie allie all come free

At first I didn't know what was happening, who was calling. I had seldom heard my father's voice above a whisper or a grumble.

He gathered us, Margaret and David and me, around the table. He told us to close our eyes.

David looked suspicious. "Why?"

Margaret grabbed my hand and dug her stubby fingernails into my palm.

"It's Valentine's Day," my father said, as if we had a tradition.

"Uh-oh," David said. Father seldom ate with us, let alone brought treats.

"See, this is what's wrong with this family. No one believes in fun." He yanked open the freezer. "Damn it, bring your moping and your bad attitudes over here and sit down! I have a Valentine treat."

The treat was ice cream—Neapolitan—a blend of chocolate, vanilla, and strawberry. David lifted his bowl and sniffed.

"Wait until we say grace," my father reminded us.

We crossed ourselves and recited, "In the name of the Father and of the Son and of the Holy Ghost."

While we prayed Tommy circled the underside of the table on his hands and knees, pulling on our hems and pinching our legs. I slapped him playfully, and he moved on to David.

David kicked him away lightly, like a pesky puppy, and he moved on to Margaret. Margaret, generous by nature, scooped a big spoonful of ice cream and lowered it under the table. Tommy squealed, grabbed the spoon, and then yanked on my skirt demanding more. When I ignored him, Tommy poked his head up over the edge of the table right next to our father's bowl and howled.

"Jesus Christ!" he shouted. "Where the hell did *he* come from?"

David loved this.

"Father," he said, "may I introduce your youngest son, Thomas, also known as Dog Boy. Thomas, this is your father. Bark hello."

Father glared at Tommy and pointed to an empty chair. "Sit."

Tommy ignored him.

"This is unacceptable."

Tommy grinned and scooped up some of my father's ice cream with his fingers.

Father grabbed Tommy's hand before he could stick it in his mouth. Tommy started to squirm and twist, but Father didn't let go.

"What the hell is going on here?" We stared at our bowls.

"I demand an answer."

"It's just Tommy, Dad. That's how he is. Don't worry." Margaret shoved her bowl toward Father. "You can have mine."

Father still had a grip on Tommy's fingers and now he was trying to pull him up into a chair. Tommy screamed. David started barking.

"Young man, you will come to the table and you will sit in a chair like the rest of your family."

With all the strength of his four-year-old body, Tommy managed to wrench his hand away and scamper under the rungs of my chair. Father tried to bend and grab him, but he wasn't limber and I circled my legs around the chair, corralling Tommy.

"Can't you just leave him alone?" David asked. "The kid just wants some ice cream."

Tommy was whimpering softly now, like a wounded puppy. He had twisted my sock around his fingers and was sucking it. When Father leaned over and saw this, his face turned deep red and he yelled at David.

"We do not live like animals in my house."

David poured Hershey's chocolate syrup on his ice cream and ignored him, so he turned to me.

"Rose, make your brother sit in a chair."

I knew it was impossible, but the safest thing was to do what I was told. "Tommy," I leaned down to speak to him under my chair. "Tommy, come sit by me. I'll give you some ice cream."

Margaret, who had been silently finishing her ice cream, quietly set her spoon down and spoke softly. "You're all crazy. He can't do what you say." She got down on her hands and knees now, smiled at Tommy and crossed her eyes.

Tommy laughed with delight.

"He can and he will." Father eased his large body down to the floor in an attempt to reach Tommy himself. "The damn kid is what? Four years old?" Tommy scooted further under the table.

"Rose," he barked. "Tell your brother to sit at the table."

Margaret stood and shouted, "I said, he can't hear!"

Everyone looked at her now and the talking stopped, except for Tommy's little whimpers.

Mother ambled in, dressed in her bra and panties and bare feet.

"Oh my, Margaret, you're getting so nice and tall. Look, Rose, she'll be as tall as you before you know it."

David laughed. "Oh god, oh god, oh god. I can't wait until I'm sixteen. I'm out of here."

Father was undistracted by Mother's arrival. "What do you mean he can't hear?"

Margaret, perhaps encouraged by Mother's appraisal of her growth, pulled herself up tall and spoke in the clearest, loudest voice I had ever heard her use. "He. Can't. Hear. Period."

Mother smiled. "Period. He can't hear. Period. Margaret." She was pouring herself a cup of cold coffee. "You're so smart. So tall and so smart. Isn't she smart, Rose, to know how to use periods at her age."

David was looking back and forth from Margaret, to Mother, to Father, and then to me. He slapped his forehead with his hand.

"Jesus," he said. "Jesus Christ."

"Rose, be sure to put a bowl of ice cream down for Tommy," Mother said. Father glared at her.

"You knew about this, Mary? About his eating under the table?"

Mother smiled and spoke patiently. "Oh, Frank. Don't be silly. Everyone knows he likes to eat under the table."

There was a long silence and then, although I tried to control myself, I started to snicker. I knew it was wrong and made no sense, but I didn't think I could stop. I covered my mouth and nose and pretended I was coughing. I said a quick silent prayer: Holy Mary, Mother of God, please don't let me laugh. Adults hate when anyone laughs at the wrong time, especially when they are angry. I knew if I laughed all the fury in the room would find me. The prayer helped a little, I nearly had it swallowed, but when I saw David's shoulders trembling, I let out a loud, barky, laughy cough.

Father scowled at me, but he looked confused. "What the hell is wrong with this family? What the hell is going on?"

"Did I miss something funny?" Mother asked sincerely, her eyes wide and hopeful. Father had started to jab his finger into the empty chair.

"He can hear and he will hear and he will sit here." Jab, jab. "And from now on, he will do exactly as he is told." He shouted as if his insistence and anger were enough to fix everything.

"Jesus," David said.

Meanwhile, Tommy scampered away to another of his other hiding places, perhaps under the end table in the living room, or in the broom closet or under a bed. He hadn't heard us, but he knew to take shelter until he was no longer the center of attention.

"Jesus," David repeated. He shook his head as if understanding this for the first time. "Margaret's right. Why didn't we know this?" He pounded the heel of his hand against his forehead. "The kid can't hear a word we've been saying. My brother isn't a dog after all. He's deaf." He rose from the table.

"I have to find him. Tommy! Where the hell did you go?" He shook his head and laughed, realizing why Tommy couldn't answer.

Mother sunk into David's empty chair. "Why is everyone going as soon as I get here? Frank, did you tell everyone the good news? Did you tell them you're leaving for San Diego?"

Father looked at Mother and then took her hand and spoke to her in a strange voice I had never heard from him. He sounded sort of sweet and sort of like he wanted to know, like it was a question, like he was asking, do you know how to juggle?

"Mary," he said. "Mary, my love, can you please put on your clothes?"

12

VELVEETA

We must follow the example of Jesus, our Good
Shepherd. When He left home to do the work for
which He came to earth, He had no money. He
lived in poverty. And He died naked on the cross
after the soldiers had taken his poor clothing.

Baltimore Catechism: The Truths of Our
Catholic Faith

While Paris rummaged in the refrigerator I licked my finger and dipped it in the sugar. Their kitchen table was so clean it shined, and there was never anything on it but a saltshaker and the sugar bowl.

"I know what you're doing," Paris said over her shoulder. "If you want sugar, just pour some into your hand, but don't be putting your spit in the bowl. That contaminates it. We'll all get polio or something."

"I don't have any diseases," I said.

Paris whipped around. "How do you know? Just let me see your hands."

I reluctantly held them out, ashamed of the black rimming my chewed fingernails.

"Uh huh. You smell bad, too. You need a bath when you get home. But for now, lick the sugar, then wash those hands." She set a box of cheese on the table. "You'll like this Velveeta. You can spread it." She opened a bag of Wonder Bread and showed me how to slice the cheese and spread it on the bread.

"What's really good is my mother's grilled cheese. Have you ever had that?"

I bit into the soft bread and oily cheese.

"Eat all you want. We've got as much as we can eat. I've only got Otis to share with and he won't eat anything that's not white. Bread, potatoes, mashed-up apples if they're peeled, rice, cream of wheat, he even likes cauliflower and that's nasty. But it's white so he doesn't mind." Paris caught me staring at the package of bread. She pushed it toward me.

"Have all you want," she said.

"Mother says you're too skinny and asked who's been feeding you?" I pulled out three slices and put cheese slices on them.

"I sure don't know how a girl as skinny as you packs away so much food."

Otis cried in the other room.

"He's waking from his nap. I better go get him." Her mother had left Paris in charge for a few minutes, just while she went to the P.X.

"I have to change his diaper. P.U."

While Paris talked and cooed to little Otis in the other room, I quickly made several sandwiches and stuffed them into my coat pockets. Paris came back with her brother balanced on her hip.

"If this baby gets any bigger he's going to blow up. Like a balloon with too much air."

I looked at little Otis. It was true, his cheeks were fat and rosy and he was happy.

It was just past four o'clock and already nearly dark. Paris rolled a slice of bread between her palms.

"Otis loves bread balls," she said.

"I better get going," I edged toward the door. "I have to make dinner tonight." I tried to slip into my coat without Paris noticing the bulging pockets.

"You take all the sandwiches you want." Paris held the door for me.

"What?" I said, as I ran down the front steps.

Bless me, Father, for I have sinned. I stole five times and I lied to my best friend.

13

INDULGENCES

Indulgences act on our soul as a washing machine acts on our clothes. Indulgences do not forgive sin, but help clean away the selfishness that is often there even after the sin has been forgiven. They are not as helpful as troubles and tribulations for making our souls grow in love, but they are very helpful to cleanse us.

Baltimore Catechism: The Truths of Our Catholic Faith

"Y ou think your shit doesn't stink like everyone else's."

My mother was yelling at David. Margaret and I and even Tommy huddled together in the bathroom doorway and watched. David had somehow squeezed in between the toilet and the wall and was shielding his head with his arms. My mother grabbed his hair and tried to shove his face into the water but he gripped the sides of the toilet seat and she was no match for him.

"Well, it does stink. Your shit does stink," she repeated over and over again.

"Stop, Mom," he mumbled, turning his face and resting his cheek against the toilet seat. "Please, Mom."

She clawed at his hand and finally forced his face into the water. "I'm so goddamn sick of your holier than thou attitude," she screamed.

"Stop it, Mommy," Margaret whimpered. Fortunately my mother and David were making too much noise for her to be heard, and I clamped my hand over her mouth before she could repeat it. Tommy was smiling and laughing his dumb boy laugh and pointing. "Huh huh," he sputtered.

"Shhh," I said, and looked at him severely. He gave me a questioning look and pointed, as if I didn't see what was so funny.

"Margaret," I whispered, "Take Tommy downstairs."

She shook her head. No!

"It's okay," I said. "I'll stay here."

"Rose." Mother had spotted me. "Rose, bring me a washcloth." And to David she said, "I'll wash your face, all right. You think you're so pure."

I did not bring the cloth. I walked away.

Bless me, Father, for I have sinned. I disobeyed my mother one time.

I turned up the volume until we couldn't hear the shouting upstairs and squeezed between Margaret and

Tommy on the sofa. On T.V. Samantha wiggled her nose and *voila*—the table was set: glasses with stems, tall white candles, and a steaming roast.

"Oh Darren," she called in a singsong voice. A smiling husband with stick-out ears appeared in the doorway.

"Oh man, Sam." He sat at the table, tucked a napkin into his collar, and smacked his lips.

Margaret's stomach growled. Darren lifted his knife and fork.

"Is magic real?" Margaret asked.

Upstairs the yelling and crying had stopped and doors slammed shut.

"Magic? No," I said. "Don't be an idiot."

On the playground I just about wanted to beat Margaret up. She had a little kid with orange hair cornered in the schoolyard and she was yelling at him. He was crying— "Leave me alone!" His feet were braced and his knees were bent and he was squirming with all his might. This kid wasn't going to take it, but she grabbed his arm and I knew Margaret. She was as strong as a bear and when she needed to, she wouldn't let go. I ran over, thinking maybe the kid had made fun of her. Called her Smelly Melly.

"Margaret, stop it," I said, when I heard what she was saying.

"You think your shit doesn't stink," she said. Dirty tears streaked his freckled cheeks.

"Margaret! Leave him alone. Do you want to get our whole family in trouble?"

She looked up and must have been either happy to see me or proud of herself, because she smiled until her dimples showed. The kid yanked his arm free.

"And if you dare tell I'll beat you up."

The kid tried to run off but slammed into me, tripped, regained his balance and ran on, wiping green snot on his sweater sleeve.

I didn't try to stop him. I knew this kid. He wouldn't tell. We were safe.

I had a piece of gum I had stolen from Theresa Tierney's coat pocket in the cloakroom. I would give it to him after school, just in case.

Margaret picked up a baseball card he had dropped, inspected it, folded it in half twice, stuck it in her mouth, bit hard, and threw it down.

I was called to the office. Sister Mary Michael, the one we called Sister Mikey, or sometimes just Mikey, because we weren't afraid of her, smiled and greeted me by my name.

"Miss Concannon," she said, and she might as well have said, "Hello, sweetie pie," her voice was so nice. I pushed my hands so deep into my sweater that my pockets stretched. Mikey only smiled brighter at this.

"Here, dear, let me see," she said, and she offered her hands, as small and plump as a baby's, with clipped, dirt-free nails. She meant for me to take my hands out of my pockets and place them in hers.

My knuckles were rough and cracked and dirty. Mikey rubbed her thumb across the sore spots.

"How long have you had this rash?"

I shook my head.

"It looks like you've had it for quite some time."

I didn't know. I didn't do it on purpose. I felt hot and my stomach dropped. I stared at my hands. They looked old and cracked inside Sister's immaculate pink ones.

Bless me, Father, for I have sinned, it has been one week. What sin? What sin had I committed? Extreme Unction? No, that was a sacrament. Adultery?

I pulled my hands free and squeezed my nail stubs into my palms.

"We really must do something about this," Mikey was saying.

Bless me, Father, for I have sinned. I didn't try my best two times.

I nibbled a sore inside my cheek to fight back my tears, and then faced Mikey.

"I'm sorry, S'ter."

Mikey averted her eyes, as if sensing my embarrassment, but continued smiling.

"Come, dear. Wash your hands. This soap won't sting. We'll put something on to help this clear up. Then we'll have a little talk."

A bone to pick. That was what my father always called it. Never a little talk. Come here; sit down. We have a bone to pick. A refrigerator door left ajar, a fingerprint on a cupboard, someone forgot to flush, poop on the seat, a squashed pea under the table, and a clump of dirt on the rug, a missing toothpaste cap, or something brand new. Why didn't anyone ever empty the garbage? It's time you kids start carrying your own weight around here. People in this family need to start making their beds. Who's leaving all the lights on? Your mother needs more help around here. Empty rooms, garbage, poop, your mother, burning lamps, rotting fruit. The list of bone pickers was long, unpredictable, and the anger was excessive. Put away the ketchup. Clean the hairs off the soap. Lately, David had started muttering bone pickers under his breath, whenever we were summoned. Me'n Margaret encouraged him with snickers. Did someone forget to fart, he would whisper? Did someone forget to kick the dog? Our father would haul off and hit any one of us for even the slightest smirk, but this didn't stop us. We all thought our shit didn't stink.

Mikey had said a little talk, what was that?

Gray, soapy water swirled down the drain. I hoped she wouldn't call in David and Margaret. I tried to remember the last time I had reminded Margaret to wash her hands. My hands left gray streaks on the white towel. My face burned with shame.

"The Lord made dirt, too," Mikey said softly.

All Mikey said after that was, "I hear your mother brought home another little bundle of joy from heaven." I left the office with a shopping bag of canned foods. Mikey said the convent provided this for all the families with new babies. When I peeked in the bag and spotted two cans of Chef Boyardee spaghetti with meatballs, I almost wished Mother would have new babies more often.

I bumped into David on my way back to class. He was coming out of the boy's bathroom and he was wearing different pants, shorter, so his socks showed, and baggier.

"Nice pants," I said.

He shoved past me, bumping me with his elbow.

He was carrying a bag, too, but it didn't look like food. Lately I had been finding his wet pants stuffed in the bottom of the laundry hamper. He always rinsed them out first, but I could still smell urine.

After school I caught up with the kid. I pressed him up against the chain link fence and threatened him with my fist. "You ever tell on Margaret, I'll kill you. Got it?"

He nodded and stuttered okay. I gave him my stick of gum and let him go. I had forgotten he was a stutterer.

14

THE CLUB OF SECRET THINGS

*Test your love of God by your love for others. Are
you kind in speech and action; helpful, generous, forgiving, even to those you don't like?*

*Baltimore Catechism: The Truths of Our
Catholic Faith*

After Valentine's Day, Mother had to go back to
Western Washington State Hospital and Father
had to go to San Diego for his new job. We were
left with relatives. There were too many of us for one family, so they split us up. Margaret and Baby Elise and Tommy
went to stay with Mother's older sister and her husband.
They had five other kids; there was no room for David
and me. Mother's little sister, Aunt Katie, a piano teacher, agreed to stay with us until things returned to normal

or until someone else could take us. Father only kept in touch when he sent the monthly check.

Aunt Katie moved in and we began living like nothing I had ever heard of, like everyday was Christmas Eve—with expectations, surprises, and a sort of miserable-happy restlessness all mixed up together. She opened the curtains and washed the windows and ordered out for Chinese food—egg foo yung, chop suey, and sweet and sour pork—and every day she played jazz on her blue portable Decca record player.

David stayed in his room.

Listen to this, she would say. Thelonius Monk, John Coltrane, Billie Holiday. Do you love it, she would ask, believing it impossible to disagree. I don't know, I might say. It's sort of—different. She might leap up at this kind of comment, her eyes shining like I had shared the most astute insight she had ever heard. Yes, yes, exactly, it is so, so different. You are brilliant, she would say, nodding, and she would squeeze my face between her ringed fingers and kiss my cold cheeks. Brilliant! But just wait, she might say, skipping over and flipping through her stack of records: Since you like different, sit, listen to this, Rose. She might grin conspiratorially then, as if she were about to let me stay up way past my bedtime. "Not just anyone will dig this." She would then slide a record from the sleeve and blow the dust from the surface. "This, dear Rose, is Miles Davis!" She would carefully place the record on the turntable, set the arm down, turn the volume up, and grin at me, never blinking until I grinned back, and soon her

eyes would no longer see me, even though she was looking straight at me, and I would sit there, locked into her
eyes, until the song was over. Yeah, I had learned to say,
oh yeah, and I would nod my head knowingly. At this her
eyes would refocus; she would smile and release me from
her stare. I knew you would like it, she would say, as she
carefully lifted the arm from the vinyl disc. There's more
where this came from, Rose.

"But tell me, Rose. Tell me all about you. What music
do you like?" she asked every time.

The only music I fully knew was a lullaby Mother used
to sing when she tucked me in at night, long ago, before
the babies were born. I still used to sing it to myself to
sleep: Toura Loura Loura.

"I really like all your music," I would always say.

"We better get the soup started. Want to help?"

I learned to peel potatoes and chop onions.

Every day after school Aunt Katie cheerily ordered me to
sit at the kitchen table and eat a melted cheese sandwich
or soup or hot toast and melted butter and she would sit
across from me and smile and insist that I tell her about
my day. Usually all I said was "nothing" because I was
bored and in a bad mood and no one had ever asked me
questions like this before. She would just smile and say—
some days are like that—and she would add—but not
mine, oh Rose, the most marvelous thing happened, *you*

will appreciate this—and she would say "you" as if I were somebody, and she would touch me lightly on my fore-arm, which of course made me feel like a charter member of the Club of Those Who Know Secret Things, and off she would go, telling me what she had done that day and whatever it was— shopping at the butcher's, posting a let-ter, going to the library—she told the truth: it had been marvelous.

One morning Sister snuck up behind me and whispered in my ear, "Miss Concannon, is something the matter? You have been awfully subdued lately."

The matter was that I was no longer jiggling my foot as much, biting my fingernails or drumming my fingers on my desk. Aunt Katie had promised me that if I stopped biting my nails, she would buy me some red Revlon nail polish. I didn't even have to try; after she had been with us for several weeks, my nails started to grow without any effort on my part. I had even stopped twisting out my hair at the nape of my neck and Aunt Katie had promised to bring me some ribbons to celebrate. All this and yet I still couldn't sleep with the lamp off. I missed Mother, I missed Margaret and little Elise, and I even missed Tommy and his sticky cheeks.

I felt ashamed for missing them.

Bless me, Father, for I have sinned.

Every night Aunt Katie would come into my bedroom and even though I pretended to be asleep, she would sit on the edge of my bed and talk to me.

"It's okay, Rose. Everything will be all right. It's just for a little while, until your mother is better."

I wanted her to stay forever and repeat this until it bounced like an echo, and I wanted her to quit telling her lies and go away. The longer she stayed and the better she took care of us, the less likely it seemed that Mother would return. Sometimes I nearly purred when Aunt Katie stroked my head, but when she tried to kiss me goodnight, I would turn away and press my face into my pillow.

"Rose, Rose," as if she could hear inside my brain, "I know you miss your mother, but it's okay to kiss me good-night; she won't mind. I promise you. I'm only here because your mother said to make sure someone is kissing you good night and tucking you in while she is away. And besides, Rose, she knows you're saving your very best kisses for her."

She would take my book and put it on the bedside table and turn out the light and kiss me on each cheek and on the forehead and tuck my blankets around me and pat me on the arm.

"There," she would say. "There, Sweetie. You'll sleep better without the light on."

I kept my eyes squeezed shut through all of this because to look her in the eye while she said such things was unbearable, like something you wanted to love and scratch at the same time, but when she turned to leave my eyes popped open and I watched her back as she stepped into the brightly lit hallway and then, as soon as I heard her footsteps go downstairs, I would turn the light on again and bury my head under the pillow and whisper, "Please don't go away."

Why did I cry myself to sleep every night when I had so much? I wondered how to confess this restlessness in confession, but I couldn't find a sin on the list that described my condition.

I supposed there were probably still some sins that hadn't been named yet.

II

Delinquency

15

THE BLUE ARMY

While we say prayers of the rosary, we try to
think of our Blessed Lord. We try to look at Him
through Our Lady's eyes and to understand
Him with her heart. While we say each group of
prayers, we think of one of the mysteries of His
birth, passion, and glory. If we notice our mind
wandering, we bring it back to the mystery. As
long as we are doing our best, the rosary is well
said, even though we have distractions.

Baltimore Catechism: The Truths of Our
Catholic Faith

If I looked at Paris with her big, wide-mouthed yawns, I would yawn, too. The long warm spring days dragged on so long I struggled not to fall out of my chair. I propped my heavy head on my hands and fought to keep my eyes open.

Sister, who was walking up and down the aisles, reading us a story from *The Book of Miracles*, paused beside my desk and leaned in close to my face.

"Miss Concannon," she whispered. I tried not to flinch at her hot dry breath. "Please sit up straight."

I lifted my head and folded my hands in my lap. Paris muttered under her breath. "A person can't even rest their head around here."

"A comment for the class, Miss Jones?" Paris jumped to her feet.

"No, S'ter, sorry S'ter. I was looking for my eraser."

Sister smiled slightly and nodded. Paris took her seat and Sister continued her rounds, and even though I didn't look I knew Paris was making holy face. I could see it even with my eyes squeezed shut. Please not today, I prayed. I really want to make it to three o'clock without getting in trouble. I straightened my shoulders and stared straight ahead. If I looked at Danny, I would giggle. I glued my eyes on the crucifix hanging above the chalkboard in the front of the room.

I prayed silently. "Dear Lord, please, please, please don't let me fall asleep. Please, I beg of you. I'll pray the rosary every night if you will just keep me awake."

Danny was trying his best to get my attention.

"Psst." I ignored him.

"Psst." I could feel a giggle starting in my chest.

"Please, Jesus," I whispered aloud.

"Psst."

I closed my eyes but kept my head up high and my face forward.

Danny couldn't stop. He had to have my attention. He yawned loudly, imitating Paris, and even dared to stretch his arms over his head, like a sleepy gorilla. Sister shot him a suspicious look and he whispered, "Excuse me, S'ter."

Sister was beginning another miracle story, her favorite, she told us.

Paris yawned again.

Although Mary, the Mother of Jesus, had made countless visitations to people on the earth, Sister told us, especially to those of the Catholic faith, the visitation at Fatima was the most recent and, perhaps, the most compelling. In May of 1917 in Fatima, Portugal, three children— Francisco, Jacinta, and Lucia—were out tending their sheep when Our Lady appeared. The visitation started as a powerful wind and a blinding light; then a beautiful woman appeared.

I closed my eyes and tried to imagine Mother cloaked in blue, but instead I saw Aunt Katie's face. I opened my eyes and stared at my desk.

This was a real modern-day miracle, Sister told us. That it had happened to three children and that one of them, Lucia, was our age, eleven, made it important. Additionally, Lucia was still alive, which in itself seemed a sort of proof. The Virgin had appeared three times. Thousands of the faithful had witnessed her second and third visitations and although her personage was visible to the children alone, many reported seeing impossible and dazzling movements of the sun across the sky.

"Aliens," Danny whispered. I squeezed my eyes shut again.

The Virgin had spoken and told secrets and passed notes to the children. She told them that Catholics the world over must pray the rosary every day to save the world from Communism. She said that sin was so serious that even little Francisco, who was only seven at the time, had enough sins on his soul already to condemn him to burn in Purgatory until the end of the world unless he started praying the rosary right then.

She also left an earth-shattering message with strict instructions that it was to be kept secret, protected in the Vatican, until the year 2000 when the Pope alone could read it. Sister raised her eyebrows and folded her hands.

"Many of you will someday be fortunate enough to learn what Our Lady's message says."

Everyone started talking. Paris turned around and Danny and I leaned across the aisle.

"I wonder about that secret note," Paris said. "I sure would like to know."

"It's sort of scary," I said.

"Not if you pray the rosary," Paris said, "like the Lady told them."

Danny grinned mischievously and said, "I bet the Pope read it already."

"He can't," Paris said. "He has to do what the Lady said."

"If I were the Pope I would just read it. Who could resist," he said.

"That's why you ain't the Pope," Paris said.

"I sure wonder what that note says," I said.

"I can hardly wait till 2000," Paris said.

"Probably about the end of the world," Danny said. "How we get blown to smithereens for being such bullies."

Before we could elaborate further on all the marvelous and horrible possibilities of the contents of the Virgin's note, Sister clapped her hands. "Boys and Girls! Please. Compose yourselves. This is not public school."

Sister then passed out brochures illustrated with a picture of three children in a mountainous region on their knees before a tall woman dressed in blue and gold. The tallest child, Lucia, had a lace mantle over her hair.

Danny examined the picture, then reached over and tapped Paris's picture with his finger.

"Look," he whispered. "Praying sheep." It was true, even the sheep were on their knees before the beautiful woman. Paris laughed loudly and Sister spun around.

"Miss Jones, we do not talk out of turn in this classroom. Now please share with the class what is so funny."

Paris stood abruptly. "Sorry, S'ter. Nothing, S'ter."

"Be seated then, Miss Jones. And please conduct yourself appropriately."

"Yes, S'ter," Paris said, lowering herself onto her bench.

As soon as Paris was seated I knew she was looking my way doing it again. I struggled to avoid eye contact at all costs or I would burst out laughing. I began foraging in my desk for a pencil. I couldn't afford to draw attention to myself. Any notice of me was usually followed by an inquiry about my family. This didn't always happen immediately, not on the spot, but later Sister would query me, as if she had just remembered my existence. It was better, safer, to stay invisible. I found my pencil and tried to ignore Paris's breathing, a deep rapid puffing in and out of her nostrils—our signal for attention. I heard it. I could picture her nostrils flaring in and out, more rapidly with each puff. I felt a laugh forming in the pit of my stomach. I turned my face to the left, away from her, careful not to allow even a glimpse of the edge of her uniform, for this was all it took to know she was practicing holy face posture. Huff, puff, huff, puff. My shoulders were starting to shake. I could hear Paris opening a book and even this, the particular, exacting sound of the cover hitting her desk top, had the sound to it. I studied my pencil tip. I scraped it with my thumbnail and turned it round and round. I knew exactly how Paris would look if I glanced in her direction. Her eyes would be downcast and her cheeks slightly darkened, a sign of shame and humility. Her eyeballs, beneath the Saint Theresa downcast lids, however, would be crossed. If I even so much as glanced her way, even saw her from the back, I would explode in a torrent of giggles. Her breathing sped up, huff puff, in and out, look at me, Rose, huff puff. I felt my throat starting to tighten. The laughter was moving up quickly. I had to get away from her before I barked out a big hoot of laughter and Sister would turn to me with her little wire-framed glasses flashing. The laughter was in my face now.

I raised my hand and sputtered, "S'ter, I need to sharpen my pencil." Sister looked at me suspiciously, but nodded her assent. I plugged my nose, the last attempt to hold it in, and stumbled toward the pencil sharpener. When I got there I realized I had left my pencil on my desk, but Paris had it in her hand and was bringing it to me. Paris did the face at least once daily to make me laugh. She could do the funniest things and somehow never be seen. She said it was easy since Sister's vision was impaired by the heavy starched wimple and thick black veil that circled her face. Danny said of course Sister knew what Paris was doing, she knew what we all were doing, she knew everything, the word for this was omniscience, and lots of nuns seemed to have this talent, even though the Pope was the only Catholic to have it officially. Danny said Paris was lucky because Sister just didn't like to be bothered with her too much.

"She just looks at you now and then to warn the rest of us," he had said. "But what you do and how you turn out, she doesn't care. The rest of us are supposed to be good Catholics, but you're colored, so it doesn't matter so much."

Paris handed me my pencil. I accepted it but still avoided her face. She walked back to her desk and I took a deep breath and found my composure returning. I turned the sharpener handle quickly, relieved that the grinding of the metal on wood was enough to disguise my snickers.

When I returned to my desk, Paris leaned over with her little cross-eyed face and grinned.

"Have you composed yourself, Miss Concannon?" she whispered. Sister wheeled around, but Paris was as quick as a cat and by the time Sister had aimed her stare, there she sat, hands folded and Sister not close enough to notice the crossed eyeballs under her humble downcast lids.

Danny was busy decorating his sheep picture with cartoon dialogue bubbles. He passed it to me. Over the children's heads he had written, "Pray, pray, pray, blah, blah, blah" and over the sheep, he had written "Pray, pray, pray, bah, bah, bah."

Sister continued handing out the brochures. A few children were giggling and whispering bah, bah, bah.

"Although you may not know what the Virgin's message says," Sister said, "you can send your own message to the Virgin." She explained that for one dollar we could join the Blue Army. We were to fill out the form with our name and address and check the pledge to promise to say the rosary every day with our families, just as Our Lady of Fatima had said we must. Once we had donated one dollar our memberships would be buried at the holy visitation site of Fatima with the other members of the Blue Army. We would be sent further information, too, in case our parents wanted to go to the Blue Army meetings. The groups were called cells, just like Communist cells, Sister explained, but instead of meeting to plot ungodly anti-Catholic things as the atheist Communists did, Our Lady's Society of the Blue Army prayed and figured out ways to stop the spread of atheism and Communism.

"There is nothing the Communists desire more, Boys and Girls, than to stop the spread of the Holy Roman faith. The way you can help is to send your dollar, talk to your parents about Our Lady's request, and pray."

"I wish I had a dollar," Paris said, picking at the scab on her pointy little knee.

I nodded. One dollar was more money than I had ever had at once, except when I'd been sent to the store to buy groceries.

"I sure would like to join up for that Blue Army," she said.

We could also help raise money by making rosaries to sell. Sister had rosary kits that we could check out and take home. The kits consisted of wire, tiny sharp scissors, colorful beveled glass beads, jewelers' pliers, and a crucifix. The profits would help send missionaries to under-privileged countries to baptize the pagans before the Communists got there and brainwashed them.

"In my old school, if we needed money, we sold candy bars," Paris whispered. "Hey, do you want to make some of those holy rosaries at my house after school? We've got lots to eat, too."

On the way home from school Paris pulled a bag of candy from her coat pocket.

"Want Kits?" She handed me a pack of four square candies wrapped like little birthday presents in yellow paper. "Banana tastes awful," she said. I had never had banana or any other flavor of Kits. I unwrapped small, pillow-shaped taffy, tossed it in my mouth, and chewed. Heaven.

"I've got more, if you like those Kits," Paris said. I smiled and nodded yes, unable to speak, my teeth glued shut with the sticky candy.

"How much do these cost?" I asked, thinking maybe I had seen them in the candy counter at Mrs. Wade's store.

"I get three for one cent," Paris said. "They've got pink, that's strawberry, chocolate, and these—banana. My daddy's in the army, so we shop the P.X. If you're army, your family can go there. You can get anything you want at the P.X. At a regular store, they cost more."

"I wish my father was in the army," I said, as I unwrapped another Kit, "so I could get things at the P.X. too." We hadn't heard from him in months.

"No, you don't wish that," Paris said. "My daddy said he has to go to war."

"What war?" I said. "There isn't a war."

"Vietnam," Paris nodded her head. "My daddy said nobody really knows about it yet, but we're sending our army over there. Vietnam. It's not exactly a war, yet, it's just a conflict, that's what they say. But my daddy's got lots of buddies over there already. One even got killed. My daddy's going pretty soon. To fight the Communists." I looked at her wondering if she looked scared, or sad, but before I could be sure her beautiful smile broke out.

"Hey, look. For my birthday, my mother got this at the P.X." She lifted up her pleated uniform skirt to reveal a ruffled blue petticoat with a tiny blue satin flower at the hem.

"Does Sister know you wore that to school?" I said.

Paris looked at me, the dumbest girl she had ever met, put her hands on her hips, and asked, "Now how is Sister going to know about my under-things?"

"Well, it makes your skirt stick out."

"How my skirt do what my skirt do isn't none of that old nun's business," Paris said, adding a little swish to her walk, taking advantage of her enhanced skirt to show how little she cared.

"I had to," I whispered.

"What're you talking about?" Paris said.

"Last year. I had to. Sister made me go in the coat closet and show her. She said I smelled bad and she needed to see if my underpants were clean."

Paris's mouth dropped open and then laughed. "You mean that old lady made you show your business?"

"My underwear," I repeated.

Paris was shaking her head now and giggling. "Rose," she said, "you know that's not right." She offered me another pack of banana Kits.

"You don't smell that bad," she said.

"Well, we didn't have a washing machine before, so I had to wear the same ones sometimes. But then we got a washing machine and now I can do our laundry every day. So," I shrugged, "I guess I don't smell anymore. Anyway, now my aunt lives with us, so I don't have to all the time, but I'm just used to it, I guess. Besides, she doesn't really know how. She turned my brother's white school shirts pink."

Paris smiled at me and put her arm around me. "You don't smell at all." She laughed and then stuck her nose in my hair. "Nope, no smell." She started to sniff me all over, my neck, my sleeves, my stomach.

I pushed her away. "Quit smelling me," I said, but I was laughing, too. I was walking home with my best friend, eating candy and laughing and telling secrets. I could not believe my luck.

We walked the next block in comfortable silence, just chewing our candy, and then Paris said, "I never heard of a kid that washed their own clothes before. "

"You never had to? Never ever?"

"No, stupid, my mother does that for me and so does everyone else's." She stopped and thought for a moment, then shook her head. "Nope, everybody's mother washes their clothes. Everybody except you and that crazy girl, I guess."

"Crazy girl?"

Her mouth dropped wide. "That girl who don't talk? Don't do anything? Bridget? She so quiet maybe you didn't even notice her."

"Bridget O'Faolain," I held my breath. Notice her? I wanted to be her. "You know her?"

"She lives right next door," Paris said. "I feel sorry for her. I really do."

Paris's house was bright and clean, with yellow curtains in the kitchen, and it even smelled like lemons. When she opened the door her mother smiled and hugged her and told her how she was happy to see her and how she hoped she had had a fine day at school and how she wished she had learned something worth knowing. She didn't bother with stupid questions about what did you learn today and did you turn in your homework and did you obey Sister. Just wishes, just hope.

Paris put her hand around my shoulders and introduced me to her mother. She said, "Mother, this is the white girl I told you about, my best friend at school. Her name is Rose." I was dazzled. I was someone worth telling about. I was a best friend at school.

Mrs. Jones smiled and looked me in the eye. "Rose, I am so happy to meet you at last."

She said she had to get the baby dressed, so we should help ourselves to sandwiches and milk. I could hear the baby crying in the other room.

"Otis. He's only two, but he's got a big mouth," Paris said.

I looked at her and smiled and suddenly, before I could think it over and stop myself, I circled her with both arms and squeezed her and kissed her on the mouth. She pulled away and looked at me like I was crazy and I knew I had gone too far and I expected her to say, "What you do that crazy thing for?"

Instead she smiled back and said, "Okay! Let's go make those holy rosaries."

16

TALKING WITH GOD

Be obedient for the love of Jesus. Especially when it is hard.

Baltimore Catechism: The Truths of Our Catholic Faith

We were dipping graham crackers into cold milk and then as they melted and broke apart, rushing them into our mouths. Slime was dripping down our chins. Aunt Katie looked up from the handmade rosaries we had spread before her. They were our fundraiser for The Blue Army.

Aunt Katie smiled. "It's hard to believe little piggies like you two could make such lovely rosaries."

Paris snorted and we disintegrated into giggles. When Aunt Katie had asked what the fundraiser was for, I was vague. School stuff, I told her. I had quickly learned not to say too much about school to Aunt Katie. She has opinions about nearly everything and it didn't take her any time at all to call Sister Superior and voice them.

✍

We had made a dozen glass-beaded rosaries in every color: red, green, turquoise, pink, clear, purple, even black. We had already sold one to Paris's mother and now Aunt Katie had promised to buy two or more. For one dollar each it was a bargain she couldn't possibly resist.

"Pretty." She picked up one, then another circle of beads, oohing and aahing like they were something made in France. She looked at Paris.

"What color would you buy?"

Red, of course. Mother would have picked red, but I didn't say this.

"Well, what do you think, Rose? What should I choose?"

I usually liked that Aunt Katie wanted my opinion, except when I didn't have one, because she never gave up. Once I had answered a question with I don't care and she had laughed, but spoke seriously.

"Of course you have an opinion. You've just not been asked for it enough. You've had way too much practice regurgitating the right answer." She shook her head. "Rose, you're a smart girl. I just wish...Rose, Catholic school is probably the worst thing in the world for a bright young mind like yours."

I think my face changed at this comment, because she quickly added, "Oh, Rose. It's going to be okay. Don't worry. We can save you. You just need more practice listening to yourself."

Margaret's favorite color was pink. David's was blue. Tommy liked anything shiny. I didn't know Aunt Katie's favorite color. She usually wore black.

Aunt Katie held a rosary to the light. "Should I get green?"

"Depends what color you like for praying." Paris said.

Aunt Katie laughed. "Oh, sweetheart, I don't want them for praying."

Paris looked confused. "What else would you use them for? I guess they make nice presents." She slurped a milk-soggy graham cracker, and licked her fingers. "What do you call these crackers again?"

"Graham crackers." Aunt Katie held a rosary of pink beads toward the window, fingering it as if it were made of rubies. "If I hang them in a window, they can be prisms and we'll have rainbows all over the house."

"No offense, ma'am," Paris said, "but I don't think you're supposed to use holy things for decorations."

Aunt Katie smiled a mile-wide smile at Paris.

"Oh, honey. They're not really holy things. They're made of glass. Things aren't holy. They have no meaning at all. It's just how we think of them, what meanings we assign them. You're what is sacred."

Paris shook her head vigorously. "My mother told me every time she prays with Grandma Nellie's rosary, what she wants comes true. She had it in her fingers when she died. They were going to bury it with her, too, but my mother said it glowed from the coffin and she knew right then to keep it. She knew it was Grandma telling us to pray for her soul." Paris looked as if she might cry, and Aunt Katie looked like she might cry herself.

Mother had saved my grandparents' funeral rosaries, too. They were wrapped in tissue paper and stored in a painted trunk. Mother pulled them out occasionally, in troubled times, she told us, when she needed extra strength for her prayers. They were the most sacred things she owned, she said.

"Paris, honey, I am so sorry. The rosary you're describing, your grandmother's rosary, the one she held when she died, that rosary is holy."

"We haven't heard anything from my daddy," Paris said suddenly.

"Where's your daddy, Paris?"

"Vietnam. We're in a war there only my mother says nobody believes it yet. My daddy got sent and we haven't heard anything. Pretty soon everybody will know about it because President Johnson's got to send more soldiers."

Aunt Katie stared at Paris as if she was something broken and she needed to figure out a repair. Paris started to squirm and pick at a scab on her knuckle.

"Everybody says there's no war. Even the president says it. It makes me crazy. I would feel better, if people at least knew my daddy was there."

Aunt Katie reached across the table and covered Paris's hands with her own.

"My mother says we've got to pray for him but I want to write the president, ask if he knows where my daddy is. Do you know how to do that? How to write the president?"

"Yes, yes I do. I think that's a very good idea." Aunt Katie was looking through her albums. "But for now, I'll put on a record. Music can give you peace of mind."

"That's what my mother said about talking to God. She said talking to God gives you peace of mind."

"Ah, here it is." She pulled a record out of its sleeve. "Listen to this, because, you know what? Sometimes God talks back. Listen." She put the record on the turntable.

"John Coltrane."

17

CHEMICALS

*How does a Catholic sin against faith? A
Catholic sins against faith by not believing what
God has revealed and by taking part in non-
Catholic worship.*

*Baltimore Catechism: The Truths of Our
Catholic Faith*

Aunt Katie taught me how to scour the bathroom
sink and tub with Comet cleanser. I sprinkled
the pale green powder into the sink, mixed it
with water, which made a slick paste, then left it to "do
its magic" for a few minutes, while I vacuumed the living
room rug. The next step was the most important ingredi-
ent, Aunt Katie said. I had to apply "elbow grease." As I
swirled the sponge around and around, the brown stains
began to fade to yellow and then disappear. After I rinsed

the sink with clear water, I polished it with a soft, dry rag, torn from my old throw away-pajamas. When I was done the sink looked as white and shiny as something new. Next I went to work on the toilet. This required rubber gloves and ammonia. The sharp smell stung my nose and made my eyes water.

While we bustled around the house sweeping and dusting and scrubbing and tidying up, throwing trash away and hiding clutter, we watched Queen for a Day. The host, Jack Bailey, was telling the most tired looking of the three tired-looking women what she had won. A pretty, happy lady, who looked just like Miss Murphy—the lady who had carried away my sister Lucille—had planted a crown on the winner's head.

"Not only will you receive a year's worth of laundry detergent," Jack Bailey shouted, "and fabric softener, you will also be awarded, FREE OF CHARGE, a brand new…"— a curtain slid open—"…Maytag WASHING MACHINE!" The audience roared and clapped as the first pretty lady's twin, who stood beside the Maytag, swept her arm grandly to show the audience the gleaming white machine. With the lady beside it, it looked as desirable as a new sports car, but they only gave those away on Truth or Consequences. The audience gasped and whistled and clapped louder. The queen's face started to contort, like she couldn't decide whether to laugh or cry, and her royal crown began to slide off, but another pretty smiling lady, the triplet, who stood slightly behind her, caught it in her glove-sheathed hand without even looking, which proved she was used to this kind of thing, and put it back on top of the queen's head. As the queen surrendered to her shoulder-heaving sobs, the lady behind her pressed her happy face against the queen's unbelieving one.

Jack Bailey continued to congratulate her. "Now you can take laundry in to earn that extra income you so badly need, while your husband recuperates and, just like any other queen, you won't even have to leave the house."

Aunt Katie stopped plumping the couch pillows and gaped at the screen. "I've never really listened to this before," she said. "My God." She looked like she was about to cry along with the queen and I prepared to cry, too, until I understood that Aunt Katie was laughing.

"Jesus, Mary, and Joseph," she wiped her eyes. "No wonder she's crying. You realize how ridiculous this is, don't you?" She winked at me. "You're too smart to ever get married, aren't you, Rose?"

We were deep cleaning because Aunt Katie had invited guests for dinner. We had never had company before, but she said it was fine, it was easy. It was fun.

"We just need to make sure the toilet is clean and the food tastes good," she said.

"Are they relatives?"

"No, Rose, special friends."

"And they get to use the toilet?"

Aunt Katie left me a list of jobs to do while she went to The Pike Place Market. I was enjoying the order and efficiency of working my way down the list—dust, sweep, mop. I had turned off the T.V. and put on a Miles Davis/

George Coleman record. With this music the housework somehow felt fun, even important, and I knew when Aunt Katie got home she would tell me it looked beautiful, like a brand new house, and she would hug me and tell me I was amazing and reward me with something warm and sweet to eat.

I was just finishing putting the dishes away when she hurried in carrying bundles of vegetables and cheeses and a bouquet of wet flowers, which she handed to me and told me to "trim the stems with a sharp knife, Rose, love, and leave them in cold water with a spoonful of sugar. It'll make them last longer. We have a vase, don't we?" We did. Mother had beautiful things, wedding gifts, stored in a glass-paned cupboard and never used.

"We do, but I don't think we can use them," I said.

"Rose, beautiful things are for using. Pick a vase, Rose, let's have a party."

"What if it breaks," I said.

"Rose," she said, and she threw her arms around me and squeezed me harder than any adult had ever squeezed me before.

I found the kitchen shears in the back of a drawer behind string, corks, unopened mail, and faded ribbons saved from birthday presents. I started snipping the ends of the flowers, inhaling the bright green smell of the stems and the sweet blossoms.

"Rose, I have a secret to tell you. I've invited someone special." The only special person I knew was Monsignor Corboy, but I didn't think she meant him, and I was glad I kept my mouth shut.

"A man, Rose." She looked at me and beamed at my floral arrangement. "Oh sweetie, that looks absolutely perfect. I love dahlias, so simple, but elegant, too. The colors! It almost makes me wish I believed in God so I could compliment him on his good taste." As she said this, she pulled a few stems, one at a time, from the vase, and then reinserted them, each time tilting her head slightly to the left and squinting at the arrangement.

"You don't believe in God?" I whispered. It would have been easier to believe that she did not believe in the moon. Sometimes my mother had knelt with us at night to say our prayers. She told us the moon was a window in heaven.

"You, my love, are delightful. Some day, Rose, some day." She held my face in her hands and kissed my cheek and laughed.

I wanted to run from the room. Aunt Katie, my beautiful aunt with the long black braid and the purple eyes, was a near occasion of sin, possibly even a friend of the devil.

"Rose, the man I Invited to dinner is named Sam Cohen. He's fabulous—handsome, smart, and Rose, he's a Jew." She smiled at me.

"He is?" I didn't know there were still any Jews. I pictured an illustration I had seen in The *Baltimore Catechism*: a crowd of angry bearded men with sandaled feet, dressed in brown robes belted with ropes and delivering Jesus to

Pontius Pilate, but a modern-day Jew? In Seattle? Coming to dinner? Bringing my aunt, who maybe didn't believe in God, flowers? Not believing in Jesus was a sin; rejecting Catholicism was a sin, too, a mortal sin, I thought. Was associating with a non-believer a sin, too? Was I going to go to hell for having my Aunt Katie take care of me? What should I say to the Jew? Should I try to convert him?

"Did you say a Jew?" I asked. "Like *the Jews?*" Shivers went up my neck; I was excited and terrified to meet this man.

"He is wonderful, brilliant. A musician. I've told him all about you. He will adore you. You have an eye, Rose. An eye." She picked up the vase we had arranged and set it on the dining room table. "And just between us girls, Rose, he's the best kisser I have ever kissed." She rolled her eyes. "Oh my God, yes."

I blushed, both elated and miserable with the intimacy. I wondered how to escape. I didn't want to think about Aunt Katie kissing and especially not kissing enough to know a best kisser when she met one.

"Rose, in spite of the advice I gave about marriage, I think I could marry him, if he asks."

I wanted to ask if it was okay for Catholics to marry Jews, but after her last remarks, I wasn't even sure if Aunt Katie still qualified as Catholic. Could you still be Catholic if you didn't believe in God, as long as you practiced the sacraments?

Aunt Katie dipped a large wooden spoon into a pot of soup that had been simmering all day, blew on it, and held it out for me to taste. "Careful now, it's hot." I sipped. "Enough salt?"

I didn't know, so I said yes.

"What does it need, Rose?"

I didn't know. "More pepper," I said. Mother's cream of mushroom soup never needed salt or pepper.

She sipped a spoonful "Perfect," she said, but she sprinkled in more pepper, tasted the soup again, then smiled and nodded. "Of course, Rose, it might be best just to live together, skip the whole middle class wedding thing."

Aunt Katie lit dozens of candles throughout the house and turned off the lights. "We need music," she said. "Rose, you choose. And go tell your brother to come down. My friends will love him."

I tapped lightly on David's bedroom door and he opened it just enough to poke his scraggly-haired head out.

"Can't you read? The sign on this door applies to everyone."

"David, Aunt Katie's friends are getting here pretty soon. She wants you to meet them."

"I don't want to," he said.

"Well, I wish you would. I don't want to be the only kid. Anyway, I have to tell you something. Can I come in?"

He rolled his eyes. "Okay, but just for a minute, Rose. I'm in the middle of an experiment." He opened the door wide and the smell hit me in the face. I coughed and clapped my hand over my nose and mouth.

"Jesus! What are you doing?"

"Stink bombs." He shut his door. "So, what do you want to tell me?"

"I can't believe that smell."

He laughed. "Yeah, it's pretty good. And that one's real simple. Just scrape the sulfur from a match head, mix it with ammonia, light it on fire, and vavoom! Easy, but really effective." He folded his arms across his chest impatiently. "So, if you want to tell me something, hurry up and tell me. I have to get back to work."

"Work?"

"Yeah, I hope you're no security risk, Rose, because this is Top Secret." He looked at me suspiciously, and then whispered, "You can't breathe a word of this to anyone. I'm becoming an explosives specialist."

"What? Explosives? You mean when you hide up here, you've been making bombs?"

He grinned and scratched his pimply face. "So far I've successfully made four types."

"Jesus, you're going to blow this house up."

He laughed. "Don't worry. I know what I'm doing. So, what did you want to tell me about?"

"Aunt Katie invited a Jew to her party."

He looked at me blankly. "And?"

"A real Jew. Don't you want to meet him?"

"Oh, wow." He rolled his eyes and spoke without expression. "Maybe after that, if we want more kicks, we can go and introduce ourselves to the Lutheran family across the street."

"Well, I'm at least curious. I've never seen a Jew before."

"How do you know you haven't?"

I leaned closer and whispered, "David, that's not all. I feel sort of bad telling you this, but Aunt Katie's an atheist."

"Duh."

"You knew? Why didn't you tell me? I can't believe it. She seems so nice."

"She *is* nice." He opened the door to his room. "I can't talk anymore."

"Come on, David, I don't want to be the only kid."

"No way."

I smirked. "Aunt Katie said you might be scared."

"I hate to disappoint you, but I'm not interested enough to be scared, Rose. I've got to get back to work."

I laughed cruelly. "Work?"

"Maybe what I do seems like a joke to you now, Rose. But this isn't just child's play. This is my life's work."

"Ha!" I shouted. "Your life's work? Making bombs?"

He pressed his fingers to his lips. "Shhh."

I laughed and my voice sounded angry and cruel.

"Blowing things up is your life's work?" I wondered if I was as ugly as him.

He looked very serious; he didn't get the joke. "Yes." He retreated into his room and shut the door.

I started to walk away, then leaned against his door and said, "Tell you what. I won't say anything about your life's work if you will at least come down and say hello. You could at least do this one small thing. You want Aunt Katie to stay, don't you?"

He didn't answer.

I stormed into the kitchen and began rummaging in the cupboard for something, anything, sweet.

"Oh, there you are, Rose," Aunt Katie beamed. "I bought these for you." She handed me a white baker's bag. She had changed into an orange Mexican peasant blouse with flowers embroidered across the neckline and a turquoise flounced skirt.

"Do I look okay?" she asked, twirling around. I stared at her, trying to understand how she had the confidence to wear clothing so obviously demanding of attention.

I suspected she only wanted my approval, not my opinion, so instead of saying anything, I nodded vaguely, opened the bag and sniffed. The cookies were still slightly warm and smelled good, but I set them down on the counter. Was this atheist brainwashing?

She shrugged and then smoothed her hands over her skirt.

"Well, it is kind of bright." I wondered why she was insisting on my opinion.

"Rose, is something wrong?" She reached her hand out to smooth my hair, but I jerked my head away.

"No. I've got a lot of homework, that's all. Your dress is pretty."

She stared down at her skirt. "It's all wrong, isn't it? Too 'look-at-me.' I'm going to go change." I thought I detected the ultra-patient, slightly hurt tone I seemed to provoke in grownups, and when she left I wondered if she had slammed the door or if it had been a draft.

I pulled a cookie from the bag and bit into a soothing mouthful of sugary peanut butter and chocolate.

"I am a mean little brat. I am a mean little brat. Mean, mean, mean. Brat, brat, brat. Please, Baby Jesus, forgive me. Mea culpa, mea culpa, mea maxima culpa." I leaned against the stove finishing off the bag of cookies.

18

PUNISHMENT

Punishment means "suffering" or "tribulation."
It means being willing to accept what is diffi-
cult; that is, what we don't like. Examples are:
troubles, pain, disappointments, upset plans,
failures, lost games, heat, cold, rain, sorrows,
and so forth. When we accept these things, we
draw close to the Cross. Our Lord cleanses us
as a washing machine cleans clothes so that our
souls will be entirely clean.

Baltimore Catechism: The Truths of Our
Catholic Faith

The summer of 1964 was unusually hot. Tommy, Margaret, and Elise were supposed to be coming home, but they were still staying with Aunt Molly. The scorching, boring days seemed to last forever.

Aunt Katie bought me my own portable record player and an album by Joan Baez. I sat around my room all summer long listening to it, eating salty foods, drinking orange Crush, and feeling irritable. Some days I only moved to go check myself in the bathroom mirror about once an hour, hoping for an improvement. It seemed logical that a change for the better might occur as randomly as all the other horrifying changes seemed to have come.

The reflection that stared back at me in the glass was disappointing and embarrassing. I felt as if my looks, my face and body, were not me at all, that I was being invaded by a hostile alien force and that hidden inside this ridiculous freak the real me still lurked, perhaps not lovely, not even almost pretty, but surely normal, normal like the kind of girl you might see ringing up sweaters at The Bon Marche. I felt betrayed by unmatched ugliness, as if it were an accident or mistake. It seemed as if somehow God had forgotten who I was or had decided he didn't love me after all.

There were many problems, but the main one was that everything was the wrong size. My neck was long, my feet big and ridiculous like a duck's, my eyebrows bushy, a band of brown freckles spread across my nose, my hair was thick and frizzy, and my top front teeth overlapped the bottom row which meant I had to smile a weird deranged smile with my lips pulled over my teeth. I looked like Long-legged Alien Stork Girl from Planet Ugly. My looks had so altered since the last day of school in June that I wondered if the other kids would recognize me or know my name on the first day.

In the second week of July Paris and I both finally started our periods. Hers came first, then mine. All it took for me to start was her coming over one day and whispering "I've got to tell you something" and us going up to my bedroom and her shutting the door and smiling so bright I thought maybe her daddy had got home from Vietnam and me getting ready to kiss her I was so happy, and her saying "Get out the list" and reaching her fingers under the waistband of her blue jeans and snapping her elastic sanitary napkin belt before I could make a fool of myself. I opened my bottom dresser drawer where we kept the list hidden beneath my socks and underpants, where David would never look.

"Write down my name," she said, grinning.

"Lucky," I muttered, as I looked for a pen to write her name under the names of all the other girls in our class who we knew had started.

"The list is getting long." I must have been pouting because she put her arm around me.

"It isn't near half yet."

"I'm never going to start," I said.

"You're next," Paris assured me.

"I hope so. Aunt Katie told me girls who are good friends coincide. That means they get it at the same time. It's like that even with apes."

"Well, there you go. Now hurry up, write down my name: Paris Georgina Jones, July 9, 1964." She lifted up her blouse. "And look at this." Little nipples shaped her bra.

I didn't have breasts yet, at least nothing noticeable once I had my shirt on, but Aunt Katie had taken me to The Bon Marche last spring and bought me a trainer bra. I wrote Mother and told her this and she sent me a card with a picture of a clown. Inside it she had signed: Love, Mary (Your mother).

Aunt Katie had told me my period would be coming soon and she bought me everything I needed to be prepared. It came in a small pink striped box labeled: Young Lady. I stored it on a high shelf in the bathroom, behind the towels, where David wouldn't see it, but I took it out regularly and looked at the contents longingly: a slim, elastic sanitary belt trimmed with pink lace, a dozen teen-size Kotex, a calendar for marking my monthly cycle, and a booklet: What Every Young Woman Needs to Know. The word "woman" embarrassed me, but I liked the pretty elastic belt and longed to wear it. I had tried it on several times over my underpants in front of the mirror. I also had hair under my arms and between my legs, which the booklet explained were signs of puberty. Sadly, I had also noticed a darkening fuzz on my upper lip. The booklet didn't mention this, probably because it wasn't womanly. I was too ashamed to mention this to Aunt Katie. She was perfect and besides she liked me. I would ask my mother about it in one of my next letters, even though she wouldn't write back.

That night, after Paris went home, I was sick. I had a fever, headache, and stomach cramps and when I came down to the kitchen in the morning, still in my nightgown, Aunt Katie took one look at me, jumped up from the table where she was drinking coffee with Sam Cohen, and surrounded me protectively, like a mother bird.

"Sweetie, congratulations. Come with me," she said quietly, as she escorted me to the bathroom. I didn't catch on until she opened the cabinet and brought down the pink box. She took out the belt and a pad and demonstrated securely inserting the ends of the pad into the belt's plastic tips. I would need to change it about every three hours, she said, but because I was new I might be irregular and should check frequently so I wouldn't have an accident somewhere like school, which I knew would be the end of my life.

She took her bathrobe off the door hook and handed it to me. "Take off your everything," she said. "You'll feel better after a nice long shower."

The only person I had ever been naked in front of was Mother and that was when I was still no more than a baby.

I slipped off my nightgown and stared at a large horrifying blood-stain on the back. I had been looking forward to this day for months and now all I felt was shame and embarrassment.

"Don't tell."

"Sam didn't see," Aunt Katie reassured me. I stepped out of my underpants. I wondered if I had to throw them away.

"Lots of blood, huh?"

I nodded.

"It's normal. Don't worry." She lifted them from the floor. "The bleeding usually slows down in a few days. I'll take care of your clothes this time, but you'll need to learn how to rinse out the stains." She filled the sink with cold water and sprinkled salt on the blood.

"Soak it for a while," she said. "If it's really bad or dried, just rub in the salt a little. You might also want to consider colored underwear now, at least for this time of the month."

She told me to wrap used pads in toilet tissue and hide them in a paper bag in the waste--basket because this was none of the men's business.

I started to cry and I didn't know why. Aunt Katie smiled at me and said, "I know." When you cried around most adults they felt obligated to try to make you stop, but she was different, she wasn't afraid of tears.

"Oh, and Rose, sweetie, our moods are part of it, but usually we feel better after the first day or so." Lastly, she handed me a bottle of Midol and told me we can take two tablets for cramps or headache or that fat feeling, whenever we need it. I was a *we* now, a woman.

I had prayed the night before to my mother, even though she was alive. "Dear Mommy," I had prayed. "Paris started her period and I'm practically the only one who hasn't started yet. Please make me start before school. I don't want to be the only seventh-grader without my period. Thank you so much. If you can do this for me, I promise I won't bother you again for anything, except to tell you how much I love you and what a good Mother you are. I love you so much. And I know you'll be better soon. Goodnight, Mommy. Amen," and I made the sign of the cross.

Maybe Mother had answered my prayers. Maybe this was none of Aunt Katie's business.

"How do you feel?"

I couldn't think what to say.

Aunt Katie still came into my room every night and, even though Sam Cohen had moved in, she still took her time tucking me in.

"Everything's okay, Rose," she always said over and over, as she smoothed my hair.

I liked this.

Sometimes, after lots of hair smoothing, she would ask, "Rose, is everything okay? Want to talk?" I never knew what to say, but my silences didn't scare her away.

"It's okay, Rose, I promise. Your mother will be home. Soon. She's getting better every day." I liked this lie, but it was hard to believe when I knew she didn't.

"Rose?"

Sometimes it seemed like she was the one who needed to talk. She would settle on the edge of my bed just like we were somebody's normal mother with her normal daughter. I wanted her to stay and I wanted her to go, but I didn't want to hurt her feelings; I would turn toward the wall and sleep breathe. The longer Mother was gone, the harder I had to concentrate to conjure up the look of her face and the temperature of her hands. I wanted to go to sleep with the thought of her, instead of Aunt Katie. I didn't want Mother to feel forgotten.

"Dear blessed Mother, please get well soon."

Lyndon Johnson announced to the nation that three North Vietnamese P.T. boats had attacked the U.S. destroyer Maddox in the Gulf of Tonkin and that the U.S. would use necessary force to repel future attacks. Sam Cohen roared a big laugh-yell at this and threw a pillow at the TV.

"Liars, goddamn liars," he roared. "Fucking convenient, isn't it? Is anyone questioning the veracity of this attack? Sounds to me like a good excuse to send 100,000 more troops to Vietnam. Jesus, here we go. Katie, I'm turning the boob tube off."

Paris's brother, Little Otis Junior, had stopped asking every day, "Where's the daddy?" But, the good thing, Paris said, was that Otis had somehow learned to read. She wished her father could be home, she said, to watch little Otis acting so smart.

Little Otis Junior was only two years old. Paris was going to tell me all about it, without even bothering to ask if I wanted to hear her brag about her little fat-legged brother. It had happened at the A&P. Paris and her mother were shopping, buying things for dinner because her mother's sister Janice and her husband and their three little kids were coming to stay for a week all the way from Detroit. We never got so much good food before, Paris said, Doritos chips and grandmother's butter pecan cookies and footlong hotdogs. Little Otis Junior was sitting in the babyseat in the cart while Paris wheeled him up and down the aisles, but he was getting himself all worked up and starting to howl, Paris explained, in much more detail than I had even the slightest interest in hearing.

"So, I opened a box of Kellogg's cornflakes we had in our shopping cart and I handed it to him to make him quiet so people wouldn't think we were child-abusers. Otis stopped hollering, but didn't shut up," Paris had explained. "I almost crashed my shopping cart into a big stack of Chef Boyardee canned SpaghettiOs then, because that little kid started to read!"

"What did he read?" I asked, not at all interested in her mistaken idea, but trying my best to be polite while she finished bragging about her little pee-stinking brother.

Paris had laughed with joy. "You'll love this," she said. "He read the box of cornflakes. He read: Breakfast of Champions."

"Maybe he heard it from you," I said, even though I knew there was more to come and it would be even more impressive.

"That's exactly what I thought, but then that smart little boy started to read the ingredients. Just like you said, I thought he must have heard me. I always read the cereal box out loud at breakfast—there's nothing better to do. So I handed him the Oreo cookies to check, and guess what—same thing—Otis read the box. My mother was over talking to the butcher, so I yelled to her and told her what Otis was doing and by now he's reading all the ingredients in the Oreos and I think maybe we could get Little Otis Junior on The Captain Puget Show, the part where kids show off their talents, ballerinas, yoyo tricks, things like that."

"He could've heard it from T.V.," I said, hoping for something to discredit her story, but I was starting to believe her and I felt jealous of her and of her little brother Otis, so much smarter than Tommy.

"Guess what happened next?"

"He said it in French?" I said, feebly trying to be funny, but she stared at me, not getting the joke and quite possibly hearing the slight irritation in my voice. Sometimes we visited Tommy and Margaret on Sundays. Tommy would be five by September and he still wore diapers. Margaret told me Aunt Mollie had spanked her for wetting the bed.

"Did you ever suspect Little Otis Junior was a genius?" Paris asked.

"You're always scratching your hands," I said. Paris folded the fingers of her right culprit hand into a fist.

"Eczema. I've always had it, but it's worse now. My skin doesn't like this heat."

"Well, it's disgusting," I said.

Paris stared out the window at the bright summer day. "My skin will feel better when it snows. My daddy's supposed to come home for Christmas."

"That's a long time away. You'll be itching your bones by then," I said, hating myself more and more, but unable to stop being this way.

"Won't he be surprised about little Otis?" She started scratching again.

"He. Can't. Hear. Period," Margaret had told us. I wondered if Tommy were toilet-trained yet.

"Would you please stop it," I yelled. Paris's eyes filled with tears. My cheeks flushed. Immediately, I felt contrite for being irritable and jealous and horrible. Even if I took it to Confession, it wouldn't make Paris feel better. I tried to take her hand, but she pulled away.

"Little Otis Junior always was real smart," I said.

She wiped her snotty nose on her scaly hand.

Since Sam had practically taken over the kitchen, David had been coming down to dinner. Sam taught David how to chop and stir-fry vegetables in a wok. Cooking was a real cool and natural thing for a chemist to do. Sam Cohen seemed so normal and nice, that if Aunt Katie hadn't told me I would never have suspected he wasn't Catholic. He had majored in chemistry at Reed College in Oregon and David said this was what he would do, too. Sam had had a really good job at Dow Chemical as a pharmaceutical researcher but he quit because Dow was researching and developing chemical weapons and he didn't want anything to do with this. He even suspected, he said, that part of the reason our involvement in Vietnam was escalating was due to Dow's financial interests. Now he had a job working in the Shipscalers Union. David said he wanted to do this, too. Sam was also teaching him how to play guitar. Sometimes at night, through the wall between our bedrooms, I could hear David plunking away and singing, "*How many roads must a man walk down.*" He sounded okay.

David was more interested in chemistry than ever. Sam had given him a shelf of his old chemistry textbooks and magazines and he was learning to make various kinds of bombs and testing them out. He had made some stink bombs and smoke bombs and Sam said he should stop there, or at least stop testing them, before he got in trouble or did some real damage, but Sam didn't attempt to stop his experimentation.

When David set off an explosion in our outdoor garbage can, blowing newspapers and wrappers and smoking cans and rotting food all over the next-door neighbors' backyards, and ours I saw Aunt Katie really angry for the first time. She said if he had to be an arsonist or a bomber to at least "exercise some discretion in selecting targets."

Sam Cohen had added, "You could hurt someone."

Not long after the garbage can incident, David planted a small stink-bomb in the confessional at Saint Maighread Church during the eleven o'clock Sunday mass. I was sure Aunt Katie would explode, but she laughed when Monsignor Corboy drove over in his gray DeSoto to investigate and she provided the alibi:

He didn't do it.

Later I sat at the top of the stairs eavesdropping as she and Sam Cohen discussed Monsignor Corboy's visit. Monsignor had admitted he couldn't prove it, but he thought she, as the stand-in parent, would certainly want to know the sins of her young charges. Perhaps David hadn't committed this most grievous of sins, but he had been acting out at school in numerous other ways. Aunt Katie didn't ask what he had done; instead she had insisted that children are not capable of sin. The evil they commit is the mirror of sins committed against them. Monsignor Corboy had explained to her that according to the Catholic Church, one reaches the age of reason at seven and is thereafter capable of sin. Aunt Katie wouldn't budge on this. Then he had brought up the Sunday collection. She said he seemed more concerned about her failure to set a good example by not attending weekly Mass and contributing to the collection than he was about David's suspected delinquency. Aunt Katie wouldn't budge on this. She told Monsignor that she did not contribute to the collection because she was not one of his parishioners; however, she provided us with a weekly allowance and it was our choice how much to spend, how much to save, and how much to give away.

Monsignor next had pointed out that she had no babies at home, so there was no reason that she could not attend Mass, and Aunt Katie must have been mad by now because instead of "telling the lies they need to hear," as she sometimes encouraged me to do, or even telling him it was "a personal matter," also acceptable, she had told him the truth. She had said, "Mister Corboy"—Sam Cohen howled at this and interrupted—"Mister? You didn't call him Mister, did you? Did you really?"

"Of course. I said Mister Corboy, although the children were unfortunately baptized Catholic by my sister, and as it still seems to be the religion their parents prefer (although at this point it isn't clear if their parents give a damn), I believe it is my responsibility to expose them to a variety of options, and when I said this, Sam, he interrupted me and asked..."

"Let me guess," Sam had said. "He asked, 'What other options are there?'"

"Uh huh. And I said many options, Mister Corboy, for example, I said, I am an atheist, of which they are aware, even if they are too young to understand why, however, at this point I believe it is not my prerogative to discourage them from practicing the religion of their choice."

Sam didn't laugh at this. "Oh God, Katie." They talked for a while in lowered voices that sounded increasingly tense.

"Why do you have to be so dumb-honest," Sam said.

"I am honest because," she raised her voice again, "that man doesn't deserve the graciousness of one of my lies."

Sam continued in a lowered voice, "Katie, I love your principles, but don't be a damn fool. You could get those kids kicked out of school."

"Ha! I wish." She was yelling now. "Don't be naive! Once they get their clutches into you, they never let go."

"Katie, lower your voice. When you're a parent, you have to compromise once in a while. These children need you."

"I-am-not," she separated her words as she spoke, "going-to-lie just to satisfy some ignorant-superstitious-Catholic-priest and," she lowered her voice but I was practiced at listening to the dark and I heard, "God damned pervert."

"Katie!" Sam said, and I couldn't tell if he was trying to soothe her or reason with her.

"No, Sam. I will not pretend to be somebody I'm not to these children, who have absolutely nothing and absolutely nobody in the world who has ever been even remotely honest with them—I will not lie just to protect their right to be indoctrinated by this Catholic bullshit."

Their voices grew muffled after this, but I heard bits.

"No, of course I didn't tell him about you, Sam."

"Honesty doesn't mean full disclosure."

"I may be a fool, but I'm not a complete fool."

"Oh god, I'm a parent now."

I couldn't make out the words after that, but they started giggling and it sounded like "something something

something—a good target—something something—well if you must, remind him to do it when school's closed."

And I heard "what I love about you."

Then I heard a thump in the hallway and David's door clicked shut.

19

DELINQUENCY

*To receive the sacrament of Penance worthily we
must:*
1. Examine our conscience
2. Be sorry for our sins
3. Make up our minds not to sin again
4. Confess our sins to the priest
5. Be willing to do the penance the priest gives us

*Baltimore Catechism: The Truths of Our
Catholic Faith*

Aunt Katie had given me one of her sweaters, a bulky blue fuzzy thing I pulled on every day after school, but I had the nervous habit of picking the bottom edge apart.

"The trick here," Aunt Katie would say, peering over the glasses she wore only for sewing or mending, "is to catch up all the broken threads before the whole garment unravels. Once it goes too far you can't fix it."

Although she worked slowly and carefully, the sweater was always a little more misshapen and easier to pull apart the next time.

One thing, Rose, she said one night, you can't keep fixing things forever. There are only so many repairs in any creation.

David and Sam were playing guitars and singing while she darned.

> *If I had a hammer,*
> *I'd hammer in the morning,*

They'd been making music all night, but this was no celebration. There was no joy, just need, as if this were the only way to get through the night. We were all too tired, angry, and scared to talk, but silence was unbearable. Without saying so aloud, we needed to be together, in the same place, almost as if, if we didn't come together, if we let ourselves drift, as we usually did, to the far corners of the house, behind our shut doors, the whole thing would unravel, beyond repair.

Thou shalt not kill.

I wanted to kill David.

Dear God, forgive me. A thought is the same as if you have done the thing. Forgive me. Give me strength. Dear God, forgive me, forgive me. Michael the Archangel, give me strength. I detest all my sins, all my sins. King of the Angels, help me. I was angry with my brother one time. I wanted to kill him, one time. Help me through this night.

Sam had given David one of his old guitars and taught him to play. Playing guitar was the only thing other than chemistry and cooking David showed an interest in. He picked it up quickly and could play anything he heard now, almost effortlessly.

Now and then Aunt Katie looked up from her darning and provided harmony:

> *It's the hammer of justice,*
> *It's the bell of freedom,*

I tried to join in, whispering the last lines with them:

> *It's the song about love between my brothers and*
> *my sisters,*

When I looked around I tried to believe we were a real family, a normal family, mom, dad, sisters and brothers, clean, polite, well-fed, and happy together.

Every few minutes Aunt Katie jabbed me and whispered: sing.

I can't, I mouthed to her.

Of course you can. Everyone can sing. She had told me this many times in the past.

But I couldn't, I really couldn't, when I opened my mouth to the music all around me all I could force out was a tuneless whisper. It wasn't that I was too timid to sing; it was just that, like a songless bird, there was no music inside me.

> *Will the circle be unbroken*
> *By and by, Lord, by and by*
> *There's a better*
> *World awaiting*
> *In the sky, Lord, in the sky*

We all felt it. No one had been able to say it yet, maybe not even been able to think it outright, but David had probably ruined everything. He had set off a smoke bomb today in the boy's bathroom, right during the Morning Offering. This sing-along was just one last gasp of breath, of looking and sounding like something still in one piece, but we could all see that everything was coming apart.

Someone had smelled smoke and pulled the fire alarm, evacuating the entire school. This time there was no alibi. There were witnesses, including the janitor. And even if David hadn't been spotted, the idiot tried to hide in one of the stalls until the smoke drove him out. When he came stumbling out the basement door, coughing and trying desperately to yank his gas mask from his face, 240 students stood in the orderly, silent lines we had practiced so many times before when the fire alarm went off, now watching with the same astonished curiosity we would have shown a spaceman descending from his rocket ship. A few little kids gasped. Cool, Danny Barry said. Who is that, several asked, but I ran to David and started pounding on his chest and arm. He was still fighting with the mask buckles and couldn't defend himself from my blows.

"Stupid, stupid, stupid," I yelled.

Other than Danny's comment—wow, smoke, cool—nearly everyone remained silent, Catholic school kids well trained to behave in an emergency, waiting for further instructions. I don't know how long I stood pounding him. Everything seemed to go in slow motion. Teachers led their rows of students to the playground, but nobody played; they all leaned against the chain link fence wondering what happens to someone who sets fire to a school. No one knew yet that it was harmless. The fire engines came. The school was declared safe and everyone eventually went back to class, except David, me, and the fire chief, who gathered in the office with Sister Norbert and Mikey, until our parents arrived. In our case, Aunt Katie and Sam.

David would've been expelled immediately and sent to Greenhill School for Boys, joining the notorious McGill brothers, but Sister Mikey, the guardian angel of every scabby-kneed kid in the school, intervened. She said we should wait a day, think, and talk it over. It was serious, but also important to think. Tomorrow we would all meet again. Tomorrow we would discuss the next action. Tomorrow we would know if Monsignor Corboy was to be involved. If so, it was Greenhill almost for sure.

The McGill brothers had been in my class, but they were two years older. They were mean, but not the meanest kids at school. When they finally got in big trouble, it was a surprise to all the nuns. The McGills were neat, handsome, blonde altar boys with perfect math scores and flawless Latin, but none of the kids were surprised, not that much. We all knew they had been holding Rocket Cat races since second grade.

Rocket Cat was where they rounded up all the feral cats at the city dump, luring them with wieners, then dipped their tails into gasoline, lined them up, and set them afire. The winner was the rare cat that dashed in a straight line. Most ran in mad circles, screaming like babies, and biting their hind ends until their ears caught fire, too. We never knew what sin finally sent them to Greenhill, but it was "delinquency" we heard, not Rocket Cat. I couldn't bear to think about this now. I tried to sing.

David's voice was a low rumble, Sam's was loud and pleasantly off-key, and Katie's was as clear and clean as a crystal bell.

Aunt Katie poked her needle into a red pincushion, put this in her sewing basket, and handed me my repaired sweater.

"Good as new."

I shrugged into it.

"Thank you," I said, but my nervous fingers were already reaching for the mended spot.

No one was hurt today, Sister Norbert had said, but she was concerned about the escalating scale of David's delinquency.

"The escalating scale," Sam repeated, staring at Sister blankly, as if trying to comprehend, backtrack, count up all the possible delinquencies that were escalating, now that proof had been provided. Oh, he suddenly said. Oh.

"Alleged delinquency," Aunt Katie interrupted, unwilling, in spite of the reports of the coughing alien in the gas mask, to forsake the benefit of the doubt until David admitted his guilt.

David and I sat side by side, too awkward to look at anything but our shoes, hoping the adults would keep talking, keep arguing, anything to avoid the suffocating silence of David's misery. I felt the warmth of his body slightly touching mine, and for once he didn't scoot away.

"Alleged delinquency," Sam parroted, joining Aunt Katie's team. Whether he believed it or not, he seemed to know that if he left her stranded right now she would simply fall over.

But then David suddenly spoke up.

"Delinquency," he said. Sam looked at him with an expression less of surprise or anger than of gratitude.

"Yes," Sister said, her voice flat, non-judgmental. "Yes. We must name the problem if we are to correct it."

Aunt Katie was nodding and reaching out her hands, clenching and opening her fingers as if trying to grab a handful of air. Sam went to her and took her hands in both of his.

"Thank you, Sister," Sam said, "for your concern and support." He guided Aunt Katie to a chair. I had never until that moment noticed how slender she was, no bigger around than a girl, really. I'm bigger than her, I whispered aloud. Sister looked at me and I shook my head. Nothing. I didn't say anything.

Mikey insisted that David did not belong in a place with the more serious offenders like Timmy and Tommy McGuire; after all, this was his first known offense, but, Sister Norbert impressed on us, his behavior is serious, wrong, deliberate and, she held David's eyes, dangerous.

Dangerous, she repeated.

The least that would happen to David would be suspension for three weeks under very strict supervision. Sister called this house arrest.

"This is very serious, young man." She looked sternly at David. "We will decide by tomorrow how best to handle you and whether or not you may continue your academic year. We don't want this to ruin your life, but we must treat it as something extremely grievous."

David didn't look away or roll his eyes or snort. Instead he looked teary-eyed and he mumbled something that sounded to me like: Shit, what do I have to do to get out of here?

Sister Norbert and Sam spoke at the same time.

"Please repeat yourself, Master Concannon," Sister said, as Sam barked, "Speak up."

He had never spoken to us like a parent, let alone raised his voice. David's eyebrows shot up.

"Screw you," he muttered.

"What was that?" Sam said, abandoning Aunt Katie's side and planting himself fiercely in front of David. "What was that?"

"Nothing," David said.

David wasn't expelled; he was suspended for three weeks. This was a miracle. Sister Mikey had intervened and convinced Sister Norbert that reporting the miscreant to Monsignor Corboy, who thankfully was not present when this all happened, "would only exacerbate the poor motherless boy's troubles."

"We must offer our prayers for the poor lad," she said, with all the sincerity of a T.V. mother's love, "and ask Our Lord to keep him in His fold."

Sister Norbert, thankfully, nodded. The boy had, after all, admitted his sin.

Bless me, Father, for I have sinned. I crossed my fingers that my brother would be sent away. I'm sorry, Father, but he is going to ruin everything.

That night no one mentioned what had happened. They just sang and sang and sang until they were too tired to continue, or out of songs, or it just stopped by itself. Still no one moved for a long while. By now I had already absently picked a thread loose from Aunt Katie's mend. I tried sitting on my hands.

David snapped his guitar into his case and said the dumbest thing:

"Well, another day, another dollar," but then anything said would have been the wrong thing.

Then he stopped, clearly searching for something else to say. Finally he said: "Well, good night everyone."

Good night, we all chirped in, too cheerfully.

We all waited for him to leave. Then, and only then, as if his absence were the permission we needed to say good night to each other, Aunt Katie and Sam rose.

"Well," Aunt Katie said, "it's late."

"That it is," Sam said, following her to the stairs.

Aunt Katie snapped off the lamp and pulled the drapes and the room disappeared.

I was alone suddenly, in the dark

"Yeah, think I'll go to bed now, too," I said to the room, but I didn't move yet. I just sat staring into the perfect black, listening to the sounds from upstairs and far away: water running, footsteps, a siren, something dropping on the floor and rolling, a whispered curse, a train whistle, a night bird, and finally bedroom doors closing.

I wore my sweater to bed that night, pressing the mended spot firmly between my finger and thumb, protecting it from myself, hoping it would not unravel before morning.

In bed, I thought about David and wished he were gone.

Bless me, Father, for I have sinned. I was un-loving to my brother one time.

20

THE ANGEL TEST

*God wants us to honor His friends. He wants us
to pray to them and imitate their holy lives.*

*Baltimore Catechism: The Truths of Our
Catholic Faith*

"**D**o you want to try the angel test?"
Margaret and Tommy were home, but who
knew for how long.

Margaret was staring at me while I brushed my hair,
which I now wore in one long braid down the back, just
like Aunt Katie's.

"Looks like you haven't brushed your hair since you
left," I said.

"You remind me of Mommy," Margaret said. I scowled
at my reflection—broad forehead and narrow shoulders
that made my head look too heavy for my body.

I yanked through a tangle.

"You don't remember her."

"She was skinny like you. But pretty."

"What's the angel test?"

"It's where you can tell if your guardian angel is real." She grinned. Her two front teeth were missing.

I braided my hair and secured it with a rubber band. "Who showed you?"

"Nobody. I just know it."

The angel test was simple. You waited until everyone had gone to bed, then you sat at the top of the stairs and waited. The angels would come when they thought you were sleeping.

I agreed to try it. We settled at the top of the stairs.

"Now what?" I shifted my skinny bottom on the hard floor.

"You close your eyes and wait," she whispered.

"How long does it take?" I was wondering if I should get pillows to sit on.

"Shh. They won't come if they think you're waiting. They're shy."

"I don't know about this, Margaret."

"Shh. Close your eyes. They only come when you're asleep." Margaret looked smug with her eyes shut, waiting for an angel.

"Have you ever seen one?" I didn't know why, but I was angry.

"I've only seen their babies. They were in a little nest at the foot of my bed. They were so small at first I thought they were little cats, until I saw their wings. No one ever sees the grown ones."

"If we're asleep, how will we know they've come?"

Margaret giggled and looked amazed. "Because, silly head, you wake up back in your own bed. They carry you there and tuck you in. That's the trick. How else would you get there?"

I had waited in the night at the top of the stairs before, but not for angels. I had waited for Mother. Every time Mother came home, I believed she was here to stay. The rest of the time was just waiting time.

The last time she came was on last Christmas Eve. I had never really believed in Santa Claus, but I always waited up. Then, like the best Christmas present I had ever prayed for, I heard her voice. She was arguing with someone, maybe a taxi driver, at the front door. Eventually the door slammed shut, but the knocks continued. Then I heard Aunt Katie get up, talk to him, and probably pay him. Next came the unmistakable sound of shattering ornaments, as if the tree had fallen.

She was afraid, she complained to Aunt Katie. They didn't feed her when she was pregnant, she said. They said it was better, healthier, to have a small baby. They scolded her, made her go to Confession, made her fast, made her stay awake at night. They want the baby to die, she said.

"I have to bring the next one home. You'll help me take care of her, won't you, Kate?"

I think I fell asleep, but later I heard yelling and crying and more things breaking or being thrown. The next day Mother was gone. No one mentioned it and the tree looked in perfect order, but I was sure I had not been dreaming.

While Margaret slept, waiting for her angel, I listened to Sam and Aunt Katie downstairs, whispering in the kitchen.

Although I couldn't make out every word, I listened carefully, knowing things whispered at night were things worth knowing.

"You've seen them, Sam. So much better. Just a few days here.

"Sam, open your eyes. Scabs, rashes.

"Their father? No idea. You saw Rose. Almost happy.

"And David. Carrying Tommy today. Giving him a ride. Like normal kids."

I think I fell asleep for a while. When I awoke Margaret was gone. Her guardian angel must have come while I wasn't watching. Sam and Aunt Katie were now whisper-shouting, but Sam's voice was too low to understand.

"Sam, I know it's not perfect, not what we wanted. You said happiness isn't where you expect to find it, that no man knows what will make him happy. Sam, how can you know?

"I do not have a choice here, not an ethical choice."

A door creaked somewhere.

"Sam!"

A door closed. Someone was crying.

I squeezed my eyes shut and plugged my ears and hummed a tuneless tune until I fell asleep.

In the morning, I found Margaret asleep in the bed we now shared.

She opened her eyes and smiled.

"You see, Rose. Angels. You don't have to believe. They like you anyway."

"I don't want to be seen with you anymore, unless you let me brush your hair."

Maybe I had been dreaming because the next day Aunt Katie was smiling and making us toasted cheese sandwiches while we were trading holy cards in the kitchen. Paris had her offerings spread across the table.

"Sister said if you pray on these cards, you can get people out of Purgatory. I'll trade you one Mother Cabrini for your Saint Christopher," Paris said.

"If you trade your Rose of Lima for St. Theresa. Your turn, Margaret."

She touched each with her finger and said,

"Eenie meenie minie moe

"Catch a nigger by the toe."

Aunt Katie turned from the sink where she was drying the dishes. "Margaret! You don't say that word. Ever. Paris, I am so sorry."

Paris shrugged. "She's not talking about me. I'm not one of those." She kept her eyes glued to her holy cards.

"Margaret, never! Ever!"

Margaret started to cry.

Meanwhile, Dog Boy was nearby, sitting in a chair, acting almost normal except for the way he was tossing his head to and fro and howling. Did he have an idea or a song in his head? I knew he was profoundly deaf, he couldn't hear anything, but he seemed to enjoy making noises.

"I wonder what nothing sounds like." Paris was examining my St. Francis Assisi. "Man, I love this St. Francis."

"That's not for trade."

"I'll give you St. Theresa, Sacred Heart, and Joan of Arc."

"I'm keeping St. Francis, Paris."

Paris turned her attention to Tommy. "Do you think nothing sounds like anything? Do you think it sounds like nighttime or like sleep?"

"Sleep isn't quiet," Margaret said. "Everyone in my dreams is always yelling and screaming, making so much noise it wakes me up."

"Aah aah," Tommy sang and he snatched one of Margaret's cards.

"No, Tommy, no." She slapped him across the cheek.

"Margaret," Aunt Katie said. "Shame on you. We use words, not hitting."

"But he can't hear words," Margaret said, defiantly.

"Then use your hands." Aunt Katie tapped her index and middle finger to her thumb, the sign for no.

"He won't do what I say unless I slap him."

"Margaret, think how you would feel."

Margaret stood up on her chair and spoke in the rudest voice I ever heard a little girl use with an adult.

"I know how I would feel. I get slapped and punched every day by my cousins. And you know what?" She planted her hands on her hips. "It doesn't hurt one bit."

"My mother would send Little Otis Junior to bed without dinner if he talked back like that," Paris whispered to me. "Something's wrong with that girl. She doesn't act right."

Aunt Katie's eyes were wide, but she didn't say anything right away. She looked like she was considering what to do, as if her next move were the most important thing in the world.

Tommy reached and grabbed a card from Margaret's stack and she reached out and slapped his hand.

"You stupid little bastard," she said. "You worthless piece of dirt."

I huddled at the top of the stairs again that night, this time alone, wrapped in a thick red blanket my grandfather had sent for my tenth birthday.

"I'm keeping them," Aunt Katie whispered.

I couldn't hear what Sam said, but Aunt Katie's whispers grew more urgent.

"What? So easily? I thought you were in this with me."

A long silence followed, then, "You saw them."

Another silence, although I knew Sam was saying something. I scooted down two steps closer and I could hear a slight rumble when he spoke.

"They're using corporal punishment!" Aunt Katie said.

"I can't in good conscience

"They need their siblings.

"Not evil? She's getting that somewhere."

Sam's voice was a little louder now, but I could make out only a few words: I just can't something.

"No, I won't be quiet."

Rumbles, then her voice was very clear. "I resent that. Of course he's angry and mixed up. But I hardly think it's because I'm not a good parent. Anyway, I'm the best he has. I'm good enough."

I scooted down a few more steps, but even with my super hearing powers I still couldn't make out Sam's whisper.

"Oh, come on, quit saying that. He isn't going to blow up the house. He's very selective about his targets."

Bless me, Father, for I have sinned. I spied on grownups. I don't know what sin this is, but I think it's wrong to listen to grownups' secrets. Maybe it's a kind of stealing.

I wanted to hear the rest, but footsteps started up the stairs so I scampered off to bed.

Dear sweet Virgin Mother, please don't let them catch me spying.

The next day Sam was gone. Aunt Katie's eyes were red and swollen and she set a box of Cheerios and a pitcher of powdered milk on the table without saying a word. Tommy reached from under the table and scooped a handful of my cereal. David looked at me and lifted an eyebrow and I shook my head, no, do not whatever you do make a sarcastic comment. I pointed toward the ceiling—we would talk upstairs after breakfast.

Later I listened to Aunt Katie on the phone.

"Sam, please. I know it isn't what we talked about. We have too much to give it up so easily. Don't decide now. Take three days."

I felt sorry for her, even embarrassed, listening to her voice shrink until she was begging like someone who has given up expectations but doesn't have the confidence to leave the room.

"Sam, please," I heard her whimpering, although I thought maybe he had hung up.

"Sam. You're the one who said happiness is not the goal. Happiness is a sometimes thing, not the only thing and not necessarily the best thing."

A pause.

"What? Who? Someone who makes you happy? Who, Sam? When did this happen?"

She hung up and continued the litany. "No Sam no how when did this happen no Sam please I'll do what you want I will I'll do anything who is she what does she have that I don't have Sam she's a new love sure but that won't last oh no Sam no when did you fall in love you've been with me every day Sam when did you fall in love why didn't I see it happening why didn't I feel this you held me at night Sam it felt like love to me, oh no oh no oh no."

The next day at school when I walked past Margaret and she called her usual Rose and ran to me with her arms spread wide, I pushed her away.

"Idiot. You've ruined everything."

III

Seven Gifts

21

GOD AND HIS PERFECTIONS

*Q: What should we do when we have committed
no mortal sin since our last Confession?
A: When we have committed no mortal sin since
our last Confession we should confess our venial
sins or some sins told in a past confession, for
which we are again sorry.*

*Baltimore Catechism: The Truths of Our
Catholic Faith*

Danny Barry didn't last long on the first day of seventh grade. We began in the usual way, on our knees, reciting the Morning Offering.

After Sister Mary Anthony took roll and each of us stood, said "present," sat again, and folded our hands on our desks, she ran her finger down the list of names, then said, "Master Barry. Please stand." Danny leapt to his feet. There were sighs of relief from those who had been spared.

"Master Barry?" Sister studied him over her steel-rimmed glasses.

Everyone had changed over the summer and instead of the usual frightened silence, as Danny stood, waiting to hear his sin, the class began to fidget, then grew noisy, until Sister glared at the rows of students.

Paris whispered across the aisle, "Oh-oh. She's mean."

By now Danny had guessed why he had been singled out.

He yanked off his hat.

"Sorry, S'ter. I forgot. It was cold when I left." His black hair had grown long and was curling down over his collar. At the sight of this, there were gasps and Johnny Farrell whistled.

"Master Barry, must I remind you that this is not public school and you are an altar boy, not a musician. Now direct yourself to the office and telephone your mother. You may return once you have lowered your ears."

This drew nervous, miserable snickers. Danny's cheeks grew red, but he rapped his knuckles on my desk as he passed. I hadn't noticed before that his hair was curly. I rested my fingers over the spot he had touched on my desktop.

"Worst kind of teacher," Paris whispered. "She thinks she's funny."

"Class, take out your Catechisms and open to page sixteen, God and His Perfections, and read silently.

When you are done, you may complete the questions at the end of the chapter. Remember to head your papers properly." I was relieved. There would be no what did you do on your summer vacation in Sister Mary Anthony's class. The chalk screeched as Sister wrote on the chalkboard: September 6, 1964.

"This year we will be reviewing what we already know." I cringed.

Paris whispered, "She would be amazed what I know."

"Miss Jones?"

Paris jumped to her feet. "Huh?"

Sister glared at her.

"Miss Jones, are you a new student at Saint Maighread?"

"No, I've been here." Paris stared down at her shoes.

"Then surely you know how to respond when you are spoken to."

Paris lifted her head. "Yes, S'ter. Sorry S'ter."

"I beg you pardon, Sister," Sister Anthony corrected.

"I beg your pardon, S'ter," Paris mumbled.

"Miss Jones, please enunciate."

"I beg your pardon, SISter."

"Be seated."

Paris whispered between her fingers, "Hmmm. She sounds all nice and mean at the same time. I don't know what to think. Am I a new student? Like she doesn't know I'm at this school. What other colored girls have you seen around here?"

"Boys and Girls, this year you will be reviewing your Baltimore Catechism in preparation to receive the fourth blessed sacrament." With the stick of chalk, she tapped the word on the blackboard: Confirmation.

"Now, assuming that we will have no more disruptions, you may begin your work."

Sister then turned her attention to lifting and shaking the white chalk from her black habit.

As Danny pulled on his jacket, Sister stopped him again. "Master Barry? That jacket? Did you enlist in the military over the summer?"

Danny finished zipping his khaki green canvas jacket. "Yes, S'ter. I mean, no S'ter. My brother, Dennis, got home from 'Nam. He gave it to me."

"In addition to your ridiculous hair cut, Master Barry, please arrive dressed for school tomorrow, not combat."

Danny blushed a deep red.

"Yes, S'ter," he mumbled as he shut the door.

Paris whispered to me through her fingers. "Danny's brother got hurt in Vietnam. He told me about it in line. He can't walk any more. Did he tell you?"

I shook my head. No, I hadn't known this. I realized now it was true, we really were at war. I felt a mix of sympathy and, sinfully, envy that Danny had told this to Paris.

Sister cleared her throat so I opened my Catechism and began reading silently: *Jesus showed us that God is all good. He calmed the storm so that no harm would come to those He loved. All these qualities of God are called His perfections. He has these powers without limit.*

The room had grown so quiet all I could hear were the buzzing lights, the ticking clock, the scratching of pencils on paper, the rustle of pages being turned, and an occasional sniffle or cough. Everyone seemed to be working, so I used the opportunity to look around and see how everyone had changed over the summer. Mary Ellen Monaghan had developed breasts and her jumper pulled tight across the front, Joanne McKay didn't have wall-eye anymore, red-headed Kathleen McWayne had permed her hair, and Maurice Santini had shed his baby fat and was tall and skinny. He had put grease in his hair and you could see the tooth lines of the comb. Only Bridget O'Faolain remained unchanged. Maurice caught me looking at him and puckered his mouth into a kiss. I curled my lip into a sneer and returned to my book and read: *God can do all things.*

Paris pssted me. "His brother? Dennis? He was only seventeen."

Science tells us a storm has the power of many bombs yet with only a word Our Lord calmed the storm.

Paris pssted again. "He got a medal for being a hero. And people still say there's no war."

God is almighty.

"Psst. What are you going to choose for your confirmation name?"

I pressed my index finger to my lips, reached into my desk for my pencil, licked the tip, and read the first question.

Does God see us?

"Seventeen. Only five years older than Danny," she said.

I licked my pencil tip and wrote: *Yes, God sees us and watches over us with loving care.*

Psst.

I slammed my pencil into the groove at the top of my desk and hissed through my teeth, "Can't you just shut up and let me work? I can't afford to get in trouble."

"Miss Jones!" Sister's eyes flashed in her angelic face. "I hope you are not going to be my problem this year. I will see you at recess."

"Damn." Paris's cheeks turned dark, but I continued working, pretending not to notice.

The first day of seventh grade was the longest day of my entire life so far. We were being held hostage on Planet Boring. We punctuated sentences, reduced fractions, read about God's perfection, the importance of olives in Spain, and why heat rises.

After school Paris grabbed her coat and left without even glancing at me. I hurried after her and had to run across the street, against the safety-patrol boy's red STOP flag, to catch up.

"I'm reporting you," Billy Bagley yelled.

"Paris! Hey, Paris! Wait up," I called, but she kept walking. Finally I caught up and stepped with my right leg twice to match my pace to hers. She pretended not to notice. We walked an entire block in silence. She had new white anklets with lace trim.

"I wish we got Sister Virginia instead," I said. "This one is too strict." Paris didn't answer.

"I'm surprised Sister didn't send you home for wearing those socks," I said.

Paris started walking faster.

"Where'd you get pretty socks like that?"

"The P.X," she said. "Same as every other pretty thing I have."

We walked another block then I thought to ask, "How's Little Otis Junior doing?"

This made her smile. She stopped walking and looked at me.

"He taught himself to play piano," she said.

"Piano? How old is he?"

"Three in November." She started walking again.

I yanked a handful of leaves from a laurel hedge as we passed. "He can't play piano if he's not even three."

"That's what I thought, too. I guess no one told him about that."

"What did he play?"

"Songs Mother sings mostly. Twinkle Twinkle. Hush Little Baby. Church songs. Holy God. Come home with me if you want, hear for yourself."

I desperately wanted to go home with her, partly so I could try to be nice and make up for not sticking up for her in front of Sister today, and partly to make up for being in a terrible mood practically all summer long. But first, I wanted to know she wanted me.

"Maybe you have too much homework," I said, testing her interest.

"Mother said she's baking today. She said she's making frosted brownies."

"I'm sorry for how I acted today, Paris."

She linked her arm in mine. "Never mind."

Now that we were walking with matched pace and linked arms, we started talking about who had changed over the summer and how.

"Danny Barry looked dumb with his hair all long." I wanted both to talk about him and to conceal my interest.

Her eyes grew wide. "He likes you," she said.

I wanted to ask for details—How do you know? Did he tell you? What should I do? Are you absolutely sure? Instead, I said, "Barf."

"I saw how he tapped your desk."

"Think he'll cut his hair?"

"He looks cute," she said. "Billy Winihan is still the cutest boy in the class, but Danny is catching up. Maurice Santini isn't so ugly anymore either, but he's meaner than spit."

"I can't wait to hear Little Otis Junior play piano," I said.

"Let's take some brownies over. Cheer Danny and his brother up." She grinned slyly. "Let's ask what he's going to do about his hair."

I hoped Danny hadn't gone to the barber yet. "You heard that new Beatles song? 'Love Me Do?'"

"It's okay. Sam Cooke and Otis Redding are better singers."

"Yeah, it's not that good, kind of weird, I like it, but not that much," I said.

"It's not too bad. Want to run?" Before I could answer yes, I was already behind.

I was afraid to go to Danny's house and see his brother Dennis. What do you say to someone who's still a kid, but he's been in a war and he's been shot and he can't walk, but Danny's grandmother opened the door and smiled at us as if everything was normal and she had been expecting us and she invited us in and told us how thoughtful it was that we had brought brownies and how happy Dennis would be to know we had stopped by and how we should be sure to come back again later, but he was still recovering and sleeping right now. But Danny would be thrilled to see us. We followed her upstairs to his room where she knocked on the door before opening it a crack.

"Danny, there are two pretty girls here to see you. Can they come in?"

Danny opened the door wide.

"Hey!" He was grinning, but blocking his door.

"Hey" I said.

"We wanted to cheer up Dennis," Paris said. "We brought him some brownies. You could have some, too, though."

Paris was craning her head around Danny, trying to see into his room.

"Are you going to let us in?"

Danny blushed.

"Oh, yeah. Sure." He stepped aside. "It's sort of messy." He picked a shirt off the floor and tossed it onto a chair.

Paris walked past him and spun around.

"It's not too bad. I've seen way messier rooms than this." I waited in the doorway, still unsure if I was welcome.

"Come on," Danny laughed. "You can come in, too." He cleared a guitar from his bed and leaned it against the wall.

I sat on the edge of his bed and looked around while Danny picked clothes and papers and books from the floor and tossed them to the chair. A picture of a curly blonde-haired Christ Child hung above his bed. He had shelves stuffed with science fiction titles, stacks of *MAD* magazines next to the bed, and dozens of pencil drawings of machines taped on the walls.

"Those are good," I said.

He blushed and laughed apologetically. "Time machines."

Paris was flipping through a box of LPs and calling out the artists' names: Bob Dylan, The Supremes, Bobby Darin, The Four Tops, The Beach Boys.

"Where'd you get all these?"

"Dennis. He let me borrow his records when he went to 'Nam."

"Doesn't he want them back?" Paris asked.

"Nope. He doesn't listen to music. He just sits in the dark. He can't stand any kind of light or noise. I'm keeping them until he's better."

Danny's grandmother knocked on the door. "Danny? Please ask your guests if they would like something to eat or drink."

"I'm okay, grandmother."

She peeked her head in the door.

"Did you ask your guests?"

"You guys don't want anything, do you?"

"Daniel Barry, shame on you," his grandmother said, but not unkindly. "That is not the proper way to offer something to your guests, not to mention, the last time I looked they most certainly were not guys. Behave like a gentleman."

"Sorry, grandmother."

"Not to me. Apologize to the two young ladies."

Paris and I giggled.

"Want a coke or something?"

Paris looked at his grandmother.

"No thank you, Ma'am. I ate before I came."

I was starving.

"No thank you, Ma'am."

"What did your brother do to get hurt?" Paris asked.

"I don't know."

"Did he tell you what happened?"

"Not too much." Danny put down a *MAD* magazine he was flipping through. "I guess he was just walking."

"Just walking doesn't get a person shot," Paris said. "What magazines do you have?"

Danny's cheeks flushed. "*MAD*. It's really funny. You can borrow some."

"I wish I took one of those brownies," Paris said. "Doesn't your brother know he shouldn't walk around places where people have guns?"

Danny's cheeks turned redder. He picked up his guitar and started lightly strumming.

"They hadn't seen any combat yet. Him and his buddies just finished dinner. They were going to play hearts. Dennis goes to get his cards and Charlie shoots him."

"Who's Charlie?"

"The enemy. Vietcong."

"He probably wasn't paying attention," Paris said. She was wandering around his room, looking at everything, picking things up and putting them down.

"He was just getting his deck of cards." Danny leaned his ear close to his guitar, strummed a few times, tightened a string, and then strummed again.

"Anybody else shot?"

"Nope."

"Probably he wasn't careful. Why else would he get shot and nobody else? What did he say?"

"He was just walking." Danny's entire face and neck were deep red now, but Paris didn't seem to notice. She shook her head.

"What else did he say?"

Danny continued strumming and tuning, strumming and tuning.

"He said it was boring. They were going to play cards." He tightened another string, tested it, and then began playing a simple melody.

Paris started flipping through his albums. "Seems like he has lots of music. Do you know this?" She held up a Bob Dylan album. "Too bad he doesn't like to listen anymore. Did he say anything else?"

"He said it was pitch dark."

"Proves he wasn't careful."

"You don't know what you're talking about."

Danny didn't look up from his guitar, but I could tell he was getting mad. His face hadn't changed, but his blues eyes had turned black and the way he was playing his guitar, I thought he might bust a string.

"It took ten hours before a helicopter could get him out." Danny was fighting back tears. Paris seemed to notice this. She sat on the bed and hesitated, but it seemed she couldn't stop.

"It's a shame." She started picking at a scab on her knee. "But all I'm saying is, probably he wasn't watching himself. He should've been more careful."

Danny put his guitar aside and looked hard at her. He was clenching and unclenching his teeth, like he was trying not to say something.

Paris's voice softened and she shrugged. "Just saying."

"You don't know what you're talking about."

"Anyway, I've got to do my homework," he said, but Paris didn't budge. She had picked her scab all the way off and her knee was bleeding. She bent it to her mouth and sucked the blood.

"If he was careful, maybe he wouldn't have got shot and put in a wheelchair."

"Paris!" I finally said. "Shut up! It wasn't his fault."

Paris and Danny ignored me.

With her face pressed against her skin her voice was muffled and she still didn't look up. "Still, my daddy said he promises to be careful."

Danny stared at her and pulled his eyebrows together like he was thinking. She continued sucking her wound. He sat next to her on the bed.

"Your daddy's in Vietnam?"

She lifted her face from her leg and nodded, but didn't look at him. "I'm just saying you have to watch yourself; you have to be careful."

Danny put his arm around her.

"No reason he had to get hurt," Paris said.

"Come on, Paris," I said. "We're going."

"I didn't know about your dad," Danny said. "Shit."

Paris's eyes filled with tears. "I've been praying every night to Saint George, the patron saint for soldiers. I don't know if he hears me, though." She finally looked up at Danny. "Nobody's heard from my daddy."

"Try Joan of Arc," Danny said. "That's who my grandmother prayed to when Dennis was gone. When's your daddy supposed to get home?"

"Christmas."

"That's not long," I said.

"I'm sure your daddy's being real careful, Paris. I'm sure he'll be home. Hey, I've got an idea." Danny lifted a fat envelope off the floor and handed it to Paris. "Here. Want to see some pictures Dennis took in Vietnam?"

Paris nodded and began slowly looking through the stack of snapshots.

She smiled. "It doesn't look so dangerous there."

22

EARTHQUAKE

*He is always taking care of us and never leaves us
alone. He wants us to have some sign of what He is
doing for us. We cannot see Him, so we need signs
to help us understand His presence among us.*

*Baltimore Catechism: The Truths of Our
Catholic Faith*

The principal's office smelled like varnish and
wet wool. David, Margaret, and I waited on the
creaky wooden bench, sitting as far apart as possible, while Sister Norbert spoke quietly on the phone to
Aunt Katie. Margaret was mouth breathing and David was
grinding his teeth.

"Why are we here again?" Margaret asked, scooting
closer to me. Margaret's frizzy hair framed a tiny dirty
face. She was picking at a bug bite on her hand. David had

set fire to his math test today and then jumped out the classroom window. That's why we were here.

"Stay over there." I pointed to the corner of the bench. "And don't say anything."

David looked thin and tired. His hands were grubby and his knuckles rough.

"You won't bring Sam back," I told him. "You just keep ruining things."

He shifted on the bench, turning his back to me. His shoulders were sprinkled with dandruff.

"Total idiot," I said. Sister looked up and pressed a finger to her lips.

"Are you afraid?" Margaret asked.

"Shh. Of course not." I dug my fingernails into my palms and tried to still my kicking leg.

Aunt Katie arrived with Sister Mikey. It was the first time I had seen her out of her bathrobe in a week. With her puffy wet eyes and no lipstick, she looked hardly older than me. Sister Mikey led her to a chair.

I guess we looked like we wanted something, because Mikey offered hot chocolate. Margaret pressed the warm mug to her cheek.

Instead of describing the delinquent's latest sin, Sister Norbert spoke softly. "We will weather this together, Miss Tierney."

Aunt Katie's hands were clenched into fists.

"I'm so tired," she said.

Sister Mikey even smiled. "We can't give up. They need you. The children need all of us."

Aunt Katie's messy hair and noisy sniffles embarrassed me.

"Can I have more?" Margaret asked. She had smudges of chocolate on her upper lip.

If Tommy had just learned to eat with a spoon, if someone had just combed Margaret's hair, if David hadn't turned into the Ape from Planet Creep, if people had just acted like families do, Sam would've stayed and we wouldn't be here.

The adults talked long and politely while we sat there feeling cold and miserable.

The Church doesn't smile on single-parent homes, Sister Norbert was saying. A boy needs his father. Single women are not the sort of influence impressionable young children should have. However, we don't have an alternative at the moment. There are no other family members willing to take them in, so we will have to do our best to make do.

I looked around at us. Even Catholic Charities would reject children this ugly and hungry looking.

Why couldn't Aunt Katie just get up in the morning? She didn't have to love us anymore, but she could at least feed the little ones? What kind of person sent children to school with dirty necks and matches?

Maybe Aunt Katie didn't look as skinny and confused to Sister Norbert and Mikey as she did to me. Agreements were made. The children would stay with their aunt. The children would be provided with hot lunches at school. They would be given new used uniforms. Things would be stricter at home. They would watch family T.V. instead of playing guitar in their own rooms. They would go to bed at nine o'clock and wake up at eight. Aunt Katie would try to get Mother home. Two mothers were certainly no substitute for a mother and a father, but better than being raised by a spinster with a boyfriend.

The sisters sent us off with unhappy smiles and three bags of groceries.

Mother returned home a week later. We were in the kitchen eating pancakes. Aunt Katie was in a good mood, something I hadn't seen since Sam left. Margaret was eating her food instead of demolishing it with the back of her fork, and Tommy was sitting in a chair eating from his own plate. We looked just like somebody's family.

Suddenly the back door opened and Mother appeared. She was wearing a green dress, a pink cardigan sweater and galoshes, but no coat even though it was pouring rain.

"I have something for everyone," she said, grinning at the happy family eating breakfast. She carried a brown paper bag.

"Mary, how on earth did you get here? I was going to come get you." Aunt Katie sounded angry.

"Don't worry," Mother said. "I have presents. A little late for Christmas, but still..." She winked. "It couldn't have really been Christmas without Mother's gifts, could it?" She looked from face to face as if she expected an answer.

Aunt Katie slammed the back door. "I imagine you haven't had breakfast," she said, pouring batter into the sizzling pan.

"Oh, yes I did," Mother said. "I always like to eat out on Sunday."

She put her bag on the counter and started digging for our gifts.

She had pencils bundled in a rubber band for David. He liked math. You can't have too many pencils if you like math.

She had two dog puzzles for Tommy.

She had a blue plastic hairbrush with a taped-up handle for Margaret.

For me she had a partially used crossword puzzle book.

"There are still some good ones left," she said.

She gave Aunt Katie a nightgown.

"It needs washing, but it's pretty, don't you think?"

"I told you there's angels," Margaret said.

Mother had only been home a few days when the earthquake struck. We were running around the house, a pack of feral dogs playing a hiding and hunting game, when the room started groaning and swaying like some monster waking in the basement. Margaret grabbed hold of me and dug her fingers into my back.

"Is the house breaking?" she asked.

Tommy was balancing tiptoe on the armrest of the sofa, with his arms spread wide, airplane style.

"Bbbbbbbbb," he said, grinning as the sofa rocked.

"Is it falling down?" Margaret asked again.

"I don't know, Margaret." Aunt Katie's hands were grabbing handfuls of air.

David came running down from upstairs.

"Whoa, it's the big one." I couldn't tell if he was grinning or scared. A few of the rattling cabinet windows started to crack. Something sounded like boulders dropping on the roof.

"Mommy's things are breaking," Margaret said.

Then it stopped as suddenly as it had begun, and only then did we notice the smell from David's room.

"Fire!" he yelled, running back upstairs. Aunt Katie followed him.

"Ah!" Tommy yelled and belly-flopped off the sofa. His tooth had cut into his lip and blood was everywhere. David and Aunt Katie's shouts drowned his screams out.

Finally David yelled, "It's fine. It's over. Just the wastebasket. Just a joke." A door slammed.

I fingered Margaret's clumpy hair. There were four globs of gum stuck in close to her scalp.

Aunt Katie was in tears when she came back downstairs. She walked right past Tommy, who sat propped against the sofa licking his bloody lip.

"That boy is getting on my last nerve." She stomped into the kitchen and closed the door.

While the earth was quaking, Mother, who sat calmly on the sofa as if nothing more than the wind were blowing, smiled.

"Boys will be boys," she said, as if setting a fire in a wastebasket were nothing more serious than a boy hitting a home-run ball through a window.

I went into the kitchen after Aunt Katie.

"What happened?" I asked.

She spun around and looked at me with an ice face. "God damn it, Rose. Do you kids have to follow me absolutely everywhere? Can't I ever have a single goddamn minute alone?"

23

MORNING OFFERING

Once He has given this life, He takes care of it in each of His sheep. He feeds each one, heals its wounds, protects it from danger, and leads it to the fullness of life in heaven.

Baltimore Catechism: The Truths of Our Catholic Faith

"Danny's not absent 'cause of his hair," Paris said on Monday morning as we hung our jackets in the coatroom. "His brother Dennis? He died Friday night. My mother talked to his grandmother. An accident."

Paris set a covered bowl on the lunchroom shelf.

"Macaroni and cheese. My mother told me when someone dies you make food. Can you go with me after school?"

I didn't want to go, but I didn't want to go home, either, so I agreed.

Before we recited the Morning Offering, Sister made the announcement.

"This morning we are offering our prayers for one of our classmates, Danny Barry, and his grandmother, whose brother and grandson, Dennis, passed away this weekend.

"We also pray for the soul of Dennis, that Our Lord forgive him his sins and accept him into His fold. Please bow your heads and pray with me."

There were a few murmurs, but everyone joined in the prayer with what sounded like sincerity instead of the overly loud pretend prayers we usually recited.

"Oh Jesus, through the Immaculate Heart of Mary, I offer thee all my prayers, works, joys, and sufferings of this day."

Just like hell, the day went on for eternity. We learned about the three cardinal virtues: faith, hope, and charity, multiplied and divided fractions, read about scientists' aspirations to send rocket ships into space, and heard how Bolivia is a plateau.

Dear Lord Jesus, forgive me. Danny's brother has died and all I am thinking about are my own problems. Forgive me, Our Father, who art in Heaven. I was selfish one time.

By the time the 3:00 bell finally rang, my palms were sweating.

"Scared?" Paris asked.

"Not really." I put on my jacket and pulled the hood up.

We climbed the first three hills without talking, and then Paris read my mind.

"My mother told me nothing you say can make it better, so all you need to say is sorry. And don't ask if they want food. You can just say, 'I hope you like macaroni,' or something like that, but don't ask if they want any. Just give it to them."

Dear Jesus, why don't I care about anyone but myself? People know what to do when someone dies, but they don't know what to do when someone leaves?

When Sam had returned for Aunt Katie I was the one who opened the door. He was holding a bouquet of wet flowers. The rain plastered down his hair and he was smiling a smile I remembered. For one stupid second I thought the flowers were for me. For the next stupid second I thought he was back to stay.

"David," I hollered before even saying hello. "Sam is back."

Sam wiped his hand across his wet cheek and asked if he could come in. I grabbed him and pulled him inside.

"Wait here. Don't leave," I said.

"I have no intention," he had said at the same moment I hollered "David" again and ran to the stairs stumbling over my own feet. I pounded on David's bedroom door, then opened it a crack. He was bent over a chemistry book.

"Didn't you hear me? Why didn't you answer?"

David looked up. An overhead light reflected off his glasses.

"Excuse me," he said. "But this is my room."

"It's important. It's Sam," I said.

"I don't give a rat's ass," he said.

Nobody was talking, but except for eating his macaroni one noodle at a time, I was surprised how normal Danny seemed. I had been afraid to be around a boy whose brother had died. His grandmother didn't ask if I wanted more, she just scooped another spoonful of macaroni into my bowl. Lucky me. I always said no thank you Ma'am, if asked, although I always wanted more. Paris poured ketchup into her bowl and stirred. Danny forked his last piece into his mouth.

"I'm going to my room," he said.

When his grandmother reminded him of his manners, he flashed a smile as uncomfortable and unrecognizable as a school photo.

"Come on, if you want," he said.

Paris and Danny took hands as they started up the stairs.

I started to follow, then said, "Guess I'll see you tomorrow."

In the end it didn't matter that David hadn't come down. Sam had come only to steal Aunt Katie away. I stood there grinning as he asked. She said of course without even taking a breath to think, and still I couldn't make myself stop smiling.

She pressed Sam's bouquet to her face and told him she had missed him in the tone of voice people use when no one else is around. I realized I had turned invisible.

Dear sweet Baby Jesus, forgive me. I hated people seven times. I hope you can forgive me, but all I feel is hate. I hate Aunt Katie for staying so long, for staying until I wanted her, for staying and keeping Mother away. I hate her even more for leaving. I hate Mother for staying away so long and I hate her for returning and making Aunt Katie go. I hate Sam for leaving and I hate him for coming back. I hate David and Margaret for everything. Absolutely everything. *Oh my God, I am heartily sorry for having offended thee.*

24

REQUIEM

He was a lost sheep, badly wounded through his own fault. He found out that pleasures do not lead to happiness. He felt even lower than pigs. Then he was sorry.

Baltimore Catechism: The Truths of Our Catholic Faith

The church smelled of incense, lilies, and burnt wax. The sacristy door opened and Monsignor Corboy, dressed in black funeral vestments, entered the sanctuary followed by two altar boys. The congregation knelt and made the sign of the cross.

In nomine Patris, et Filii, et Spiritus Sancti. Amen.

I followed in my Missal.

Introibo ad altare Dei.

I will go to the altar of God.

The stuffy choir loft smelled of hot bodies. People were sniffling and their stomachs were growling. I sniffed my armpit.

We could see everything from the choir loft. The church was full except for the first three pews, where Danny and his grandmother sat alone, pressed against each other. I wondered if they knew or cared that the church was full, or if they felt like the only two people there.

Sister raised her arms and we sang, *"Requiem eternae, dona eis Domine."*

Dennis Barry's coffin sat in the center aisle, draped in the American flag. He was only eighteen, five years older than Danny. I tried to imagine how it would feel to kneel six feet from my brother's dead body. It didn't seem possible that Dennis could be in that huge dark box and Danny could be sitting there not crying or looking around or anything. Just sitting as if it were a normal thing.

When Danny and his grandmother had walked up the aisle, arms linked, everyone had stared and whispered. Danny, who usually looked around, embarrassed, when he walked, held his head up and looked straight ahead. His hair was shaved up high above his ears and his suit was too large. He looked like a boy on Halloween masquerading as a mourner. When they turned around to watch the pallbearers carry in the coffin and unfold the American flag on top, Paris jabbed me with her elbow.

"Psst."

Sister looked over with opaque glasses that were either smudgy or foggy. When she looked away, Paris poked me in the rib with her finger.

"Psst," she said. "See that? Everybody's staring to see what a boy whose brother died looks like. He's the same, only sad now. He'll never be happy all the way again."

Throughout the Mass Tommy, sitting in the last pew with my mother, Margaret, and David, called out in a loud tuneless moan.

"No reason to be embarrassed. He's singing," Paris said.

"He's deaf," I said.

"Just because he's deaf doesn't mean he's got no music in him."

꩜

After the funeral Paris asked me to go to the Barrys' house. She had been over everyday after school since Dennis died.

"I never thought someone we know could die," she said. "At least he came home from Vietnam. My Daddy's coming home soon, too."

"Sister needs me to stay and help put the music away. I'll come later," I said. I waited until everyone had left to descend the creaky choir loft stairs.

I didn't want to be around Danny with Paris. He had stopped talking, as if there were no words left in the world, and Paris couldn't leave the silence alone. When my daddy comes home I want him to meet you, she told Danny.

Somehow Dennis's death became the story of Mr. Jone's return. When my daddy comes home this and when my daddy comes home that.

Paris was waiting for me in the vestibule. "I figured you might want someone to go with you."

"I have to go home and help Mother."

"It's not contagious," Paris said.

"What are you talking about?"

Danny and his grandmother passed without noticing us and started up the hill alone with their arms still linked.

"If you're not scared, then come with me, let's walk with Danny."

"They don't want us to bother them."

"Yes, they do, that's exactly what they want. Because Danny's sad doesn't mean you have to hide from him. You don't even have to talk about it. You just have to show up."

What did that skinny little blabbermouth know about anything? Every day she went home to a mother who made her bed and ironed her shirts while she was at school.

"I told you, my mother needs me."

"When you change your mind, come over. There's lots of food, too," Paris said.

At home, Mother ranted as she opened a can of soup and plopped it in the pan.

"Those people don't give a damn about Dennis Barry. People just like to be nosy, get in people's business. No one talks to Grandmother Barry for years, and then they show up with Jell-O molds. Hell no, I'm not stopping by. Why should I show up? So everyone can ask me how I am? What the hell's that supposed to mean—how are you? How the hell are they? Don't tell anyone our business, Rose."

"Do we have business?" Margaret asked. She was ripping off pieces off toast, rolling them into balls, and arranging them around the edge of her plate like a pearl necklace.

"Did you see how that Mrs. Lenahan tried to corner me after the funeral? I couldn't see around her, let alone breathe. Do I ask her business? That woman is disturbed."

She suddenly turned on David. "Don't roll your eyes, Mister. You'll see. When you're older, you'll see. Where was everyone when Dennis was home and so lonely he hung himself? Now they're baking cookies. Hypocrites. The hell with all of them."

25

THE GIFTS OF THE HOLY GHOST

*If we trust in our Lord and work hard, He will
give us what we need.*

*Baltimore Catechism: The Truths of Our
Catholic Faith*

"The seven gifts of the Holy Ghost are wisdom,
fortitude, knowledge, piety, counsel, understanding, and fear of the Lord."

"Correct, Miss O'Faolain."

Bridget smoothed her skirt as she took her seat, relieved to have passed her Catechism exam.

Paris snorted. "That girl probably thinks those are
nice gifts. Fortitude. Knowledge. What crazy presents are
those? The Holy Ghost heaps gifts on us then tells us why
they're good. But they're no fun, they don't taste good,
and they don't bring my daddy home."

CAROLYN ROSE HALL

Danny laughed. "Yeah, where's my catcher's mitt?"

It had been three weeks since Dennis Barry's funeral. I had scarcely talked to Danny since then. He invited Paris and me over every day after school, but I was busy. Mother was still home. I worried that if I didn't take good care of her, she might not stay. Also, although I was afraid to admit it, I was afraid to be around someone whose brother had died.

"The three cardinal virtues are faith, hope, and charity."

"Well, well, Master O'Brien," Sister teased. "Please be seated."

"Phew," Timmy said.

Confirmation was on Sunday. We had final exams today and tomorrow.

"Come study after school," Paris said. "Oral Latin is the only thing left."

"And Confession." Danny laughed. "Last call for gluttony and sloth, my house today, 3:30."

Paris smacked her lips. "I hope your grandmother made more of those marshmallow dream bars."

"You coming?" The eagerness in Danny's voice scared me.

"I might be busy today," I said, chewing on a fingernail. I wondered if I would feel different once I had my new gifts from the Holy Ghost. Fortitude meant strength. Paris was wrong, this was a wonderful gift.

192

26

MAGIC WAND

We are the sheep who have fallen into danger
through our own fault. Our Blessed Lord comes
to rescue us in the Sacrament of Penance. He
stoops down from heaven to pick up His sheep
and take us out of danger.

Baltimore Catechism: The Truths of Our
Catholic Faith

O n Saturday morning, the day before Confirmation, the rain was so cold and heavy it stung my
face as I made my way to Danny's house. I had
been feeling guilty and decided it was time to see him.
My clothes were drenched through to the skin by the time
I arrived. Grandmother Barry welcomed me with a thick
towel and a cup of hot spicy cider.

"We're happy to see you this morning," she said, although Danny was not in sight. "There's still waffle batter. May I make you one?"

"No thank you, ma'am," I said, although I was hungry, as usual.

Danny and Paris were sitting cross-legged on the floor near his record player, listening to some song I didn't know. Other than the records strewn about the floor his room was neater than I had ever seen, except for the drawings taped all over his walls.

"Here to examine your conscience before Confession?" Paris laughed.

"Bless me, Father, for I have sinned. I ate too many waffles for breakfast," Danny said.

"The rain sounds like drums. Seems like winter's here again. Have a seat." Paris patted the rug and I sat between her and Danny.

"I can't wait until tomorrow. We get those seven Holy Ghost gifts. Which one do you like best? Fear of the Lord?"

Danny laughed softly and I felt him move where our arms touched slightly.

"I understand most of the gifts, except counsel," Danny said.

Paris was chewing the cuff of her sweatshirt and her voice was barely audible above the pounding rain. "That's where you supposed to tell your friends how the Catholic Church is the one true church. Like missionaries. It gives people a chance to convert."

"Are you teething?" I asked. I felt mean and critical, but she didn't take it that way. She laughed and took a big mouthful of her cuff.

"Yum." She laughed. "Nothing like an old sweatshirt. Better than your grandmother's waffles."

"I tried counsel. I wanted to practice and see what happens," Danny said softly. I thought he was joking and I waited for the funny part.

"I wasn't sure if I should because if you tell someone about Catholics and how we're the one true religion, they have to join or else it's a mortal sin. They're almost better off not knowing, but you have to give them a chance."

"Yeah, a chance to go to Sunday Mass. A chance to faint from fasting," Paris said.

"Sister said it's a chance to get into heaven," I said.

"Yeah, and play the harp with the rest of those Catholics up there." Paris looked at Danny. "Oh, you're serious."

"Who did you tell about Catholics?" I asked. I didn't know why but I felt a little jealous and also guilty for not having done the same, but the only Protestants I knew were the Bynum twins across the street and I didn't play with them much. One of them said their mother didn't want them to play with us. We were a bad influence. Trash, she said. I thought they were Lutherans.

"I told Jimmy and Luke," Danny said.

Paris snorted. "When did you do that? You're kidding."

"What did you say?" I was annoyed with Paris for laughing.

"We were playing basketball. I told them, but I made it easy. I said they could come to church with me."

Paris slugged me in the arm. "This is good. You're shooting baskets and talking about Catholics. What did they say? Did they join up? I bet they think you're from Mars."

Danny tried to smile with her. "I hope Sister isn't right. Now they know the truth, they could go to hell for not converting."

"That's a good one. Your friends come out to play basketball, and you tell them about all this Catholic voo-doo stuff, and send them to hell for not converting. Man, you've been an altar boy way too long."

"I wonder what your grandmother's making for lunch?" I said.

This made Danny laugh at last. "Didn't you just eat waffles?"

I wished I had. My stomach was growling loud enough to be heard.

I laughed, too, when Paris said her mother said I must have two hollow legs, but I felt guilty. Had everyone noticed how I was always hungry? I decided to change the subject.

"Do you miss Dennis?" I asked.

Danny jumped up. "Hey, I invented some new time machines. Take a look."

Paris elbowed me. "Shh. You not suppose to remind him." I shrugged.

Danny pointed at a tiny, complex drawing hanging on his wall. "This is a miniature one. You can tuck it in your pocket."

"You could go anywhere, anytime. For example, I could go back to when I was six years old with Dennis teaching me how to shoot baskets. Anything. All with the pull of a lever."

"If you had a magic wand and could wish for anything, any gift, what would it be?" I asked.

"Yeah, instead of those seven Holy Ghost gifts, say we get whatever we want for Confirmation." Paris made holy face and named the seven gifts: wisdom, understanding, piety, fortitude, knowledge, counsel, and fear of the Lord.

"Any wish at all?" she asked.

Danny lay back on his bed with his hands under his head. "Say it's anything. I know what I would want. That's easy. I would want to build a real time machine."

"I would want a pink petticoat and to be as smart as Little Otis Junior," Paris laughed. "No, for real? I want my daddy to come home, of course."

"It would be so cool to meet Jesus. Or Columbus. Or Robin Hood," Danny said.

"Rose, you're quiet. What would you want?" Danny asked.

"Rose?" Paris said.

I was thinking. If I could have anything, what would it be? So many of my wishes had come true. Things were great at home. Mother was home, watching soap operas, getting dressed most days and sometimes even making dinner. David hadn't been a jerk in a while. Tommy was finally potty-trained and eating with a spoon. Margaret was taking her weekly bath and even letting me comb her hair. Aunt Katie was gone, but it seemed okay, somehow. She would visit.

"You have to say your wish," Paris said. "This one doesn't come true unless you say it out loud."

"I can't think of anything," I said, but I was lying. I had thought of something. I just couldn't say it aloud.

Paris was laughing again. Her white teeth were sparkling in the dim rainy day room. I hadn't seen her so silly in a long time, and Danny had caught it and was laughing too. The rain was spraying the window with little bursting stars.

"Probably a lifetime supply of candy, the way she likes to eat," Paris said. "Or Velveeta."

"Or a lifetime supply of holy cards," Danny said.

I looked around at my friends and I laughed, too, because I knew what I wanted and my wish was coming true, right then and there.

Paris was laughing so hard she was snorting. Danny was telling her how she belonged in a pigsty, which made her laugh even harder until she fell over on the floor.

"Ooh, my stomach hurts from laughing," she said.

"Me too," I said.

Downstairs Grandmother Barry was cooking lunch and I was laughing, too, sitting in a dark room with my best friends, talking and laughing about time machines, Little Otis Junior, and the Holy Ghost, and I knew, I just knew, that my wish had come true.

27

ONE HUNDRED SINS

Confess your sins often. Jesus loves to forgive. It brings Him His greatest joy.

Baltimore Catechism: The Truths of Our Catholic Faith

I closed the door and knelt in the stuffy confessional. The screen window slid open and young Father Moffat's silhouette appeared. I made the sign of the cross.

Bless me, Father, for I have sinned.

The Lord is present. Tell me your sins, child.
Father, I don't know how to begin. Tomorrow is my Confirmation.

God understands, Child. You are here to prepare your soul for a most Holy Gift. Perhaps begin with the sins that are most troubling.

Father, it has been one week since my last Confession and I have sinned twelve times.

> *Father, it has been one week since my last Confession and I have committed twenty, thirty, maybe one hundred sins.*

My Child, God is present. He loves to forgive your sins. It gives Him His greatest joy.

Yes, Father.

I am here.
  God is present.
  Tell me your sins, Child.

> *I want to tell everything*
> *I want to have a clean soul, free of sin*
> *When I receive the Holy Spirit tomorrow*
> *I want to be as pure as a baby,*
> *No, purer than a baby, we are born into sin, the*
> *sins of Adam and Eve. So,*
> *I want to be as pure as the day I was baptized,*
> *When my original sin was washed away and*
> *I had not yet begun my life of sin.*

*I wonder if anyone ever baptized Little Lucille
and Elise.*

Father, I lied five times.

*Ten times, fifty times.
I lie all the time, Father, Bless me, Father,
I have never told the truth.
Everything I say is a lie.
I don't believe a word I say, I don't believe a thing
I do
I'm lying right now.
And oh yes, anger, that is a sin, too, one of the
seven deadly sins.*

Father, I have been angry three times.

*How many times have I really been angry?
How do I count?
I am angry all the time, all the time.
Do I count by seconds, minutes, hours, and days
of rage?
Do I count by incidents?
I wonder if there are people who are not angry.
I wonder what it would be like to be free,
to have peace of mind
and a happy heart.
Do I deserve a happy heart when I am so selfish?
I think only of myself*

I've missed my mother,
I miss Aunt Katie now,
I have so much.

Yes, Father, I have been angry three times.

So angry, I have holes in my hands, in my palms.
No, not stigmata like Our Lord.
I don't think I will be picked to be a saint, no
these are
anger holes.
I dug them myself.
They are infected now.
Aunt Katie tried to help.
Another accident, I said. Another lie.
When I try to stop digging into my skin, I bite my
fingernails.
Sister told me to stop.
Not ladylike, a filthy habit,
but I have bitten them to the quick.
This is a sin,
a sin of disobedience.
Everything I do is a sin.
Maybe that is what a sinner is.
I am a sinner.

Father, I have been disobedient two times.

Yes, Father, I see that sinning not only hurts Jesus, it hurts me, too. I will try harder.

Is that a sin, Father, to think of myself? When Jesus hung on the cross for three hours for me?

Yes, Father,

I will offer up my sufferings for the poor souls in purgatory.

Do I have sinful thoughts?

Yes, Father, I have had sinful thoughts three times.

> *I haven't been able to sleep through the night since I was seven years old. I think about everyone. I think of Little Otis Junior and his smart-mouthed sister. I wonder where Little Lucille and Elise are and when they are coming home.*
>
> *I'm jealous of Danny. Since his brother died, everyone seems to love him. He seems so happy.*

Do I have evil dreams?

Yes, Father, I have had evil dreams three times.

> *I dream my father is home and I am hitting him, just punching him until he says he will bring everyone back home for good.*
>
> *And I dream I'm screaming at my mother, but she doesn't answer. I scream and scream and she says nothing at all. She just sits there like she can't see me.*

Father, I have been unappreciative three times.

Sometimes I resented my Aunt Katie for taking care of us.

Yes, Father, yes, she is the one who was seeing the Jew.

Should I finish my Confession now?
Bless me, Father, for I have sinned.
It has been one week since my last Confession
I have sinned ten thousand times.
Bless me, Father.
It has been one week since my last Confession.
I have committed five years' worth of mortal sins.
I went to communion every Sunday with sins on
my soul.
I have lied in Confession many times, too many
to count.
I chew my fingernails and I pull out my hair.

Father, forgive me. I have been greedy three times.

I am greedy and I hide food so no one else will
take it.

No, Father, I don't always say my bedtime prayers.

Instead sometimes I squeeze and kiss my pillow
and imagine it is my mother, kissing me good-
night and tucking me in.

I wrap my arms around myself and squeeze
and squeeze and squeeze.
    Is that what you meant, Father?
    Is that a sin, Father, to wrap my arms around
my ribs and squeeze myself to sleep?

Father, these have been my sins. Lord, forgive me, for I know not what I do.

For penance say ten Our Fathers and ten Hail Marys.

Yes, Father.

Now you may recite the Act of Contrition.

Oh my God
I am heartily sorry
For having offended Thee
And I detest
All my sins
Because of Thy just punishments
But most of all
Because they offend Thee
My God
Who art all good
And deserving of all my love
I firmly resolve
With the help of Thy grace

To sin no more
And to avoid the near occasion of sin
Amen.

Go in peace, my child.
   You are forgiven.

Thank you and love to Ben Brockhaus-Hall, Hilary Brockhaus-Hall, Amontaine Aurore, Roger Anderson, Mike Cohen, Paul McCulloh, Brianna Morgan, Mike Dumovich, Karina Nyquist, Nicole Merat, Cole Holland and James Knauff. A special thank you to Shogo Ota for the cover design. Also a deep thank you to Hedgebrook on Whidbey Island.

Carolyn Rose Hall is an artist, writer, educator and pho-
tographer, living in Seattle, Washington. She is faculty at
Cornish College of the Arts and Antioch University.